The
REVENGE
OF THE
FORTY-SEVEN
SAMURAI

The

REVENGE

OF THE

FORTY-SEVEN

SAMURAI

Erik Christian Haugaard

Houghton Mifflin Company
Boston

Library of Congress Cataloging-in-Publication Data

Haugaard, Erik Christian.
    The revenge of the forty-seven samurai / by Erik Christian
Haugaard
        p.   cm.
    Summary: A fourteen-year-old serving boy finds himself surrounded
by suspicion and betrayal as his master gathers a group of samurai
to avenge Lord Asano's death.
    ISBN 0-395-70809-5
    1. Forty-seven Rōnin — Juvenile fiction.   [1. Forty-seven Rōnin —
Fiction.   2. Japan — History — Akō Vendetta, 1703 — Fiction.
3. Japan — History — Tokugawa period, 1600–1868 — Fiction.
4. Samurai — Fiction.]   I. Title.
PZ7.H286Re   1995   94-7691
[Fic] — dc20   CIP
                            AC

Printed in the United States of America
QUM 10 9 8 7 6 5 4

To my wife, Masako,
without whose help this book
would never have been written

■ ■ ■

Contents

	List of Characters	ix
	Preface	xi
1.	How It All Began	1
2.	My Master Calls a Meeting	10
3.	The Three Old Men	16
4.	Oishi Chikara	22
5.	Okajima-sama	28
6.	The Last Days in the Castle	34
7.	The Sword of Lord Asano	40
8.	The Surrender of the Castle	46
9.	The Samurai Spy	52
10.	We Move to Yamashina	59
11.	Goro	65
12.	I Am Wounded	71
13.	Otaka Gengo	77
14.	On the Road to Edo	84
15.	Two Officers of the Shogun	92
16.	The Silk-Clad Actor	98
17.	We Return to Yamashina	104
18.	A Meeting in Kyoto	110
19.	Otaka Gengo Loses His Temper	118
20.	My Master Is Divorced	124
21.	I Get a Room of My Own	130
22.	The Floating World	136

23.	Chikamatsu Monzaemon	143
24.	A Message from Edo	152
25.	My Master Eats Sashimi	158
26.	I Have a Strange Dream	163
27.	Otaka Gengo Leaves for Edo	168
28.	Chikamatsu Monzaemon Again	174
29.	I Find Out Who My Father Was	181
30.	We Return to Edo	189
31.	Otaka Gengo Masquerading as a Rich Merchant	196
32.	The Day of Revenge Is Near	203
33.	The Night Before	209
34.	The Revenge	215
Epilogue	The End of the Story	223

List of Characters

Asano Takumino-kami. Lord of Ako in the Province of Harima.

Kira Kozukenosuke. Grand Master of Ceremonies for the Shogun.

Tokugawa Tsunayoshi. Shogun ruler of Japan.

Oishi Kuranosuke. One of the chief retainers of Lord Asano, and the leader of the forty-seven samurai.

Oishi Chikara. Son of Kuranosuke, a sixteen-year-old boy.

Jiro. A servant boy to Oishi Kuranosuke, the hero of the tale.

Haru. Jiro's mother, a servant of little importance.

Matsu. Chief servant to Oishi Kuranosuke.

Yoshida Chuzaemon. Loyal retainer to Lord Asano.

Hara Soemon. Retainer of Lord Asano.

Okajima Yasoemon. Retainer of Lord Asano, fond of sake.

Ono. A disloyal chief retainer of Lord Asano.

Lord Uesugi. Son of Kira Kozukenosuke and his protector.

Goro. Acolyte in the Buddhist temple Reikonin.

Otaka Gengo. Young retainer of Lord Asano who befriends Jiro.

Ichikawa Danjuro. A famous Kabuki actor, founder of a dynasty of actors. The present one is Ichikawa Danjuro the twelfth.

Okuno Shokan. A loyal but disagreeable samurai.

Usagi. A little servant girl.

Kamoko. Servant in the floating world.

Chikamatsu Monzaemon. Playwright, sometimes called the Shakespeare of Japan.

O'Karu. A beautiful woman of the floating world.

Uma. A giant porter.

The
REVENGE
OF THE
FORTY-SEVEN
SAMURAI

·1·

How It All Began

The fly on the wall, if it could hear and see and understand what goes on, would know everything. For no one notices the fly, unless it is foolish enough to make itself known. I was such a fly, a boy of no importance. My name is Jiro, for I am the second son of my mother, Haru. Who my father was I do not know and I scarcely think that even my mother does. My older brother died at the age of three, so I am the head of the family, which consists of my mother and me. My mother was a servant to a samurai who was one of the chief counselors of the Lord of Ako. So by chance I got involved in an event the fame of which has spread to all parts of Japan.

Lord Asano, Daimyo (or Lord) of Ako, my master's master and therefore mine as well, was summoned to Edo by the Shogun. It was the third month of the fourteenth year of Genroku, a day which should have been of no importance, yet proved to be one that no one who lived in Ako castle would ever forget. Ako castle is west of Kyoto, where the Emperor lives, and more than a week's journey from Edo, where the Shogun reigns. It is a rather sleepy castle town near the sea. On that particular day the cherry trees had started to bloom and my master and his wife and children had gone out to view them, taking their lunch underneath the flowering trees.

When calamities happen and your world falls asunder, there ought to be a warning first. Lightning does not strike from a cloudless sky, nor does frost attack in a summer month. Yet that is what happened to us. A messenger came late in the evening. I heard the sound of the horse's hoofs hitting the stone pavement in front of the castle. I was not asleep (my mother and I slept in a little alcove next to the kitchen of our master). I got up to see who had come so late, for I was always eager to discover what went on. The rider stumbled as he dismounted; he was so exhausted that his legs found it difficult to carry him. He was led to the room of my master, who was in charge of the castle while Lord Asano was away. I woke my mother, as I felt certain that she would be called to furnish food for the rider, whom I had recognized as one of the samurai who had accompanied Lord Asano a month before, when he had left for Edo.

The kitchen is not in the castle itself but in the yard nearby. A stablehand was holding the samurai's horse. I went out to talk to him, but he was a surly fellow; besides he knew nothing more than that the horse had been "spoiled" by too hard a ride. As I had guessed, a servant came and demanded food for the rider and I brought up a bowl of rice and a plate with some vegetables and fish. My master, Oishi Kuranosuke, sat deep in thought, a roll of paper in his hand, the letter the messenger had brought. He was not reading but contemplating it, as if it were a live snake. I put the dishes on a small table in front of the samurai, then knelt in a corner of the room waiting to hear if anything further was wanted.

"Sake." My master looked at me, scowling as if the word itself was a curse, not a mere demand for rice wine. I brought the sake in a small pitcher with two cups.

My master pointed to the door while glancing at me. I bowed, signifying that I had understood my dismissal. As I closed the door, I heard my master say, "So all is lost."

His words echoed in my mind as I made my way back to the kitchen. "So all is lost." I repeated them to my mother, but she has no imagination and just shrugged her shoulders. I have often thought that my mother was like a packhorse, a beast of burden, whose sole ambition in life is to eat a little more and to sleep a little longer. Now she was busy, noisily eating a bowl of rice. *She is getting fatter and fatter,* I thought, trying to imagine what she must have looked like when she was my age.

"It is some news of tremendous importance he brought, something that concerned our Lord Asano," I said. My mother nodded, as her chopsticks conveyed the last grains of rice from the bowl to her mouth. " 'All is lost' may mean that the castle is lost," I added. My mother nodded again, though I don't think she even heard me; then she put the bowl away and climbed back into her bed, drawing the covers over her head. I sat for a while, waiting to hear if I should be called again, but I wasn't. Then I blew out the little oil lamp and climbed beneath my covers myself. In the darkness I thought again about the words I had heard; they didn't frighten me but excited me instead. Something was about to happen. Tomorrow would be different from today, but I didn't mind that at all, and looked forward to it.

I had just gotten up and so had the sun, when yet another messenger arrived from Edo. He, too, had ridden his poor nag nearly to death. The horse was covered in foam and sweat. The rider looked worn out, as if he couldn't have sat in the saddle much longer. He was immediately taken to my master's room. I made the fire bloom and woke my mother so that she could cook rice for the master's breakfast. My master's family does not live in the castle, they have a house nearby. But being the lord's chief advisor, he has a room in the castle, and when the daimyo is away he lives there. My mother was not the chief cook in my master's house (she was too poor a cook for that), but while he lived in the castle we served him. He was not difficult to please, which was lucky for my mother. She was happy to be there, and not back home where she was merely one of the lower maids, for here she was in charge and could indulge in her two favorite pastimes, eating and sleeping.

The rice was hardly ready when I was told to serve the breakfast. It was lucky that I had heard the rider arrive and woken my mother; if not for me she would have lost what small position she had in my master's household long ago. My one fear was that she would be sent to work on the land of a small farm that my master owned, for I would have had to go with her. I quickly brought tea and rice with some leftovers from the evening meal. As I have already said, my master was not a fussy man about his meals, and the samurai was so hungry that a bowl of millet gruel would have satisfied him. As it was, he ate two big bowls of rice. I knelt in the corner of the room near the door as silent as a mouse, but with my ears open.

"Are we now masterless?" the young samurai asked.

My master nodded as an answer but then said, "To the others we will be ronin, samurai without masters, two-sworded beggars, but to ourselves we will still be Lord Asano's retainers. The insult he received was ours as well."

"That is the way I feel, too." The young samurai's eyes shone as his hands fondled the hilt of the shorter of his swords. "If my master is dishonored, so am I."

My master, Oishi Kuranosuke, smiled and nodded in approval. "I must call a meeting of all our Lord's samurai and we must decide what to do. You go and rest, for you must be very tired. Did you see our master before he killed himself?"

"No." The young samurai shook his head. "Kataoka Gengoyemon was the only one to see him. He cannot speak about it without his eyes watering."

"Go and sleep. I have much to think about and much to do. You have done well." My master frowned at the empty dishes in front of him and I hastened to take them away.

Once back in the kitchen I said to my mother, "Lord Asano is dead! He has committed seppuku, slit his belly open."

My mother's chopsticks paused on the way to her mouth. "Who will be our master now?" she asked and continued eating.

"I don't know." I shook my head, for Lord Asano had no children. "Maybe his brother," I suggested.

My mother put her chopsticks on her now empty bowl.

"He is not much good at anything," she said with a frown. "Why did he kill himself?"

"I don't know. It has something to do with the Shogun. But it will be all over the castle before noon."

"What difference will it make to us?" My mother frowned again as she thought about the question she had asked, and then she answered it. "He won't starve, and as long as there is food for him, we won't either." Then she belched and picked her teeth with a bamboo splinter.

"Our master will only be a ronin now," I said, for I gathered that my mother's "he" meant our master, Oishi Kuranosuke.

"He has silver," she said and shrugged her shoulders and then started to wash the dishes in a pail of water I had brought.

As I thought, it did not take long before the news was all over the castle, and by noon there was no one who did not know what had happened to our master.

"He behaved as a nobleman should. That rascal Kira should lose his head," I heard one samurai say to another, who nodded in agreement.

"He was a fool. Why did he not make Kira's sleeves a little heavier? What good is silver but to spend it?" That was a stablehand's opinion, a man who probably had never owned a piece of silver and therefore was not against spending it.

"What really happened?" I asked my master's head servant, a clever and honorable man. "And what will it mean to us?"

"Jiro, as to what happened I can tell you that, but what

it will mean to us I am not so sure of. Much will depend on what action our master will take."

"I heard him agree that his master's dishonor was his," I said, recalling the words.

"Yes, that would be the way he would see it. He is faithful, but will the rest be as well?" The servant frowned and I thought, *Yes, he too is faithful, his master's fate is his.* But my mother did not care and I was not so sure that I did either. "Tell me please, what really happened?"

"Why do you want to know, Jiro? It matters not to you." The servant, whose name had been shortened to Matsu, scowled. "So long as you and your mother have well-filled stomachs you are both happy."

I knew that my mother's greed and laziness had given us a bad name in the household and that there was little I could do about it. "Maybe that's what's worrying my mother," I said, grinning as I slapped my stomach. "She fears that she will grow as thin as a pine tree."

Matsu — the name means pine tree and he was as thin as a young tree — laughed. "That would do her good, you little rascal. I will tell you what happened. You know that the Shogun had asked our master's master to be one of the two lords who were to entertain the Emperor's envoys who had come to greet him?"

I nodded. "Yes, I know that, and also that our lord did not like the job."

Matsu smiled. "Yes, Lord Asano liked the simple pleasures and had little use for all the ceremonies that ruled in the palaces of the mighty. He would sooner have stayed here in Ako than mix with such as Lord Kira. But that was not to be." Matsu shook his head in despair. "Lord Kira is the Shogun's master of ceremony, and knows exactly how low and how many times you have to bow to this or that person. He is a man whose sleeves are always open to bribes; unfortunately our Lord only sent him some dried fish, not a bucketful of silver. The Shogun had told Kira to help our master, but since his sleeves were so light that they fluttered in the breeze, he was very angry and insulted our master many times. Lord Asano bore it meekly, but at last it grew too much for him and he drew his sword and attacked and wounded Lord Kira, though it was but a slight cut that Lord Kira received. The Shogun, who is known to lose his temper easily, lost it so completely that he did not find it again. The very next day Lord Asano was forced to commit seppuku, and his name was erased from the list of the Lords of Japan. Now you know what happened."

"Who is Lord Kira — is he a daimyo, a great lord?" I asked.

"He is not, but he likes to act as if he is, or so I have been told. For that he needs a lot of silver, more than he is paid. He is a samurai of some standing, a hatamoto."

I frowned for I did not know what the word meant. "A hatamoto — is that as high a rank as a daimyo?"

"Fool, it is not. He is a samurai in the Shogun's service. They say he comes from Suruga, and is as close to the Togugawa family as you can get without bearing their name. He is an arrogant fellow whom few like, but he is well connected."

"Who will become Lord of Ako now?" I asked, a little confused.

"It won't be you and it won't be me, that is all I know, and besides that I have no time to stand here talking to the likes of you. So go and help your mother."

I obeyed and went to find my mother, telling her all that I had learned. As so often with my mother, I was not sure that she listened or heard what I said to her. When I had finished my tale, she grumbled, "What fools they all are." This was like many of my mother's sayings; I didn't know what she meant. Was it Lord Asano she had called a fool or was it Matsu or me or maybe everyone? There was no point in asking her to explain — I had tried that, but she would just shake her head or say something equally hard to make sense of.

Whatever happens, I said to myself, *this is a day of importance, to me as well as to everyone else. Nothing will be as it was before; everything will be different. I shall count everything from this date, the day that we heard that Lord Asano had died.* The samurai of the clan were masterless now, but I was not like them. Where they had much to lose, I did not. I owned nothing but the clothes on my back and they were not much better than rags.

"We are the flies on the wall," I said to my mother. She looked at me as she was cutting up a radish, then made a face and spat on the ground.

·2·

My Master
Calls a Meeting

The hall, the biggest room in the castle of Ako, is not so
very large. Here Lord Asano used to meet with the samurai
who were his retainers and owed him allegiance. It could
comfortably hold fifty or sixty men, but not much more.
My master had called a meeting of all Lord Asano's samurai,
which amounted to a little over two hundred. By taking
away the screens that divided the hall from two other rooms,
it was enlarged, but would that be enough?

"They'll have to sit as close as squids that are hung on a
stick to dry," Matsu declared, as I was helping him remove
the screens.

"Maybe they won't all come," I suggested. I thought the
main room of the castle very big and grand.

"Oh, they'll come, just as pigeons will come when you
spread grain on the ground. There is much to talk about,
and then there is the matter of money to be divided —
some will come for that alone."

"Is there much money?" I asked.

"More than you will ever see, Jiro, but not much when
divided among so many. And then there is Lord Asano's
wife — she must have her share."

"How big will our master's share be?" I asked, trying to imagine a great pile of silver coins.

"Larger than some, but smaller than others." Matsu shrugged his shoulders. "Our master is not greedy, but there are some who are."

"I'm not, but my mother is," I said and grinned. Everyone made fun of my mother, and I did too. But when I did it, I always felt rotten afterward. It was as if I had betrayed myself, but that did not prevent my doing it over and over again.

"Your mother —" Matsu shrugged his shoulders in contempt. "They won't be served anything but tea if they want it. You'll be out in the courtyard, and will serve the tea there. Our master has forbidden any servant to be present in the hall."

I nodded to show that I understood. In a castle no bigger than ours it's hard to keep a secret, and I was certain that I would get to know everything that had happened inside.

"Some of the younger ones, the older ones too, are no better than pigs," Matsu growled in a low voice. "They will do right here against the wall that which should be done out in back by the stables."

I laughed. I had never seen my master do it, but loads of times I had seen other samurai relieving themselves in the courtyard of our castle when they had been drinking sake. Being eager to get back inside to drink more, they didn't waste time by going far in order to get rid of what they had already drunk. "They usually go over there," I said, pointing to a corner where two walls met. "I can throw some water on it in the morning."

"You're a good boy, Jiro. Be obedient to our master and you may advance far." Matsu shook his head in approval of the wisdom in what he had said.

I nodded mine as well, wondering what he meant by "far." He was head servant to my master, and all he owned in the world, as far as I knew, were the clothes on his back.

"So that is what is asked of us: to fight the Shogun, which means asking to be killed." The man held out his cup for me to refill with tea.

"Not so loud," his companion whispered. "There are too many ears here, eager to listen." Then in a more normal voice he continued, "We could not hold the castle for long; still I see it would be an honorable thing to do."

"Honorable maybe, but foolish certainly. Besides, it is hardly fair to our Lord's brother. If we fight the Shogun's men when they come to take over the castle, we make certain that no one by the name of Asano will ever sleep under its roof again. Oishi thinks more highly of his own honor than of the Lord's he claims to serve." The two men walked back to the meeting in the castle. Keeping my ears open while doling out tea, I had learned everything that had taken place inside. Some of the samurai had been eager to fight and defend the castle, and to die there. Others, like the last two, had not. What would I have chosen to do, had I been a samurai? I wondered about it, but then, if I had been a samurai or the son of one, I would not have been me, but someone else. No one was going to ask Jiro, the son of the slovenly cook, if he wanted to die or not.

"Tea! Are you asleep?" I grabbed a cup and quickly filled

it, without looking up to see who had spoken. It was my master's son, Chikara. He was only two years older than I.

"Have you been in there?" I asked as I handed him the filled cup.

"Certainly. My father is going to hold the castle against the Shogun."

"I know." I nodded. "There are those who do not agree with it, though." I never knew if Chikara was going to act my master or be just another boy. It all depended on how he felt.

"Those we will do without," Chikara said haughtily. "When a samurai's Lord is insulted, then he is insulted as well, and when his Lord dies, he dies as well." Chikara struck a rather grand pose as he said this and I felt sure the words were not his own but his father's.

"How can you hold the castle against the army of the Shogun?" I said, as I refilled Chikara's cup.

"We shall hold it as long as we can, and then die defending it. That will show everyone that we have been loyal to our master." Chikara was still feeling heroic but suddenly he started to grin. "Before we give in, your mother will be cooking rats and mice."

"I suppose I'll have to catch them; how many will there be for dinner? I know of some who can't wait to eat rats," I said, taking back his cup.

"Maybe two hundred, maybe more." Chikara looked doubtfully toward the castle entrance, from which a lot of noise was to be heard.

"It's easy to be loyal when the reward for it is a full belly, but more difficult when loyalty demands that you slit it open. Holding the castle against the Shogun — is that not the same as committing seppuku?" I asked.

Chikara handed me his cup; now he was eager to get inside again. "To commit seppuku is not difficult for a true samurai." He had suddenly remembered that he was his father's son and I my mother's. "You wouldn't understand that." He grunted and walked away.

No, I wouldn't, I thought. When I had heard that our master, Lord Asano, had been ordered by the Shogun to commit seppuku, I had thought about the matter. As I went to bed I had even looked upon my naked belly and had drawn my hand across it as if it held a knife. Would it really be easier for Chikara to do it than for me? I didn't think so, but maybe I was wrong. I didn't think I could do it at all. I could imagine the blood flowing as you cut the skin. No, I couldn't do it. Was that because my mother was just the lowliest of servants and I didn't even know who my father was?

It was getting dark when the meeting ended. My master asked everyone to return the next day. I watched them leave — one samurai who had held a high position, by the name of Ono, had many followers with him. One young samurai of his company complained loudly that my master had been too arrogant. "It seems to me," he said, "that Oishi thinks himself a daimyo, the retainer who has become the master." Then he laughed loudly at his own wit.

I was cleaning up and was just about to throw some bucketfuls of water at the corner, so no smell should offend Matsu in the morning, when he came to tell me to bring some sake for three persons to my master's room.

"Will they be wanting something to eat as well?" I asked. "They must be hungry by now."

"Have your mother prepare some simple dishes and let her cook them with mountain herbs; I know our master likes that."

As I entered the room, carrying cups and sake, it grew so silent that it shouted "conspiracy" aloud. My master could not help smiling and said, "Jiro is not used to silencing his betters." This made the other two men in the room laugh. I knelt and put the cups in front of them, and then I poured the sake. I was going to serve my master first, but he pointed to the oldest of the others, a samurai named Yoshida Chuzaemon. I poured next for the other samurai; he too was an older man, Hara Soemon. I was just about to pour for my master, when Yoshida took the bottle from my hand and poured instead of me. My master smiled and bowed and then motioned with his hand that I could leave. As I slid the door to close it on my way out, I heard my master saying something which made the other two laugh.

·3·

The Three Old Men

My master, Oishi Kuranosuke, is a man who has already lived at least two scores of his life, but his two friends were even older. Yoshida-sama was so old that he had been a grandfather for some years. I knew him best, for he was very friendly and open, and would always thank me courteously when I brought him tea. It is so easy to be loved by servants; all you have to do is to treat them as if they, too, were human beings. A nod, a thank you, is a precious gift to a tired servant. To some of the samurai you did not exist, and they would never notice you unless you got in their way. There were also some who got pleasure out of mistreating you, and they were truly hated by those who served them. They were usually to be found among the lower-ranking vassals, but sometimes those whose gray hair should belie such foolishness would indulge in it as well. All three old men that I was serving that evening belonged among those whom servants served willingly.

The food my mother had prepared was better than what she usually managed to cook. I was therefore pleased when I slid open the door. For a moment my master frowned, but then, glancing at the dishes, he smiled. I arranged the dishes in front of each man and then bowed so deeply that my face touched the matted floor.

"Kuranosuke, you are well taken care of." Yoshida-sama laughed as he picked up his chopsticks.

"Yes." My master looked for a moment at me. "Jiro is very good, and I think trustworthy."

I bowed my head to indicate that I was indeed trustworthy and my master nodded.

"Trustworthiness is as important in a servant as in a samurai, but often missing in both." Hara-sama looked at me as if he were seeing me for the first time and found me worth scrutinizing. "You are a lucky boy to have a good master," he said.

Again I bowed, by this action indicating my agreement with what had been said. I knew the importance of a servant's being mute.

"Bring some more of the sake," my master ordered, and I crawled toward the door.

"More sake!" My mother smirked. I suspected that she had been drinking some herself; her cheeks were flushed. "Well, they might as well drink it as the Shogun's soldiers, having more right to it." I looked surprised at my mother. I had just filled the three little pitchers and was ready to carry them up.

"When will the Shogun's soldiers come?" I asked, wondering if the answer I would get would make sense.

"They will come when they will come," she said and scratched her head. I waited a moment to hear if she was going to say anything more, but she only laughed. *She is getting madder and madder*, I thought, as I carried the rice wine to my master and his friends.

When I returned, my mother had already lain down to sleep. I walked over and looked at her. Her eyes were closed but that did not mean that she was asleep. *She is cunning as a fox*, I thought, *and maybe she is one*. It is well known that foxes can change themselves into human beings. It is said that we must honor our parents, but why is it not said that they should behave in such a way that it is not difficult to do so? Feeling sorry for myself, I poured a cup of tea and sat down; I wanted to stay awake should my master call me.

It was late, the hour of the rat had passed by the time the two old men left. I had refilled the pitchers of sake once more and the faces of the guests were flushed and their legs unsteady. Their houses were not far from the castle. I saw them as far as the gate, where the soldier on watch bowed deeply as they passed. When I returned I was surprised to find my master waiting for me. "Come," he said, beckoning to me, and I followed him back up into the room where he had been entertaining his friends. I knelt just inside the door, wondering what he wanted with me. Surely he didn't want any more sake, though he seemed as though he had either drunk less than the other two or it had not affected him at all. Oishi Kuranosuke, my master, seated himself on the same pillow he had sat on before; then he just stared at me. I bowed my head, but as he did not speak I looked up again after a while, only to find that Oishi-sama was still contemplating me. Again I bowed my head and at last he spoke.

"Jiro," he asked, "what does it mean to be trustworthy?"

"Oishi-sama," I answered, "I am not sure what it means, for it may not mean the same to all men. To boys like me it means that we can keep a secret."

My master laughed. "Do you have many secrets, Jiro?" he asked.

"Not so many, Master, yet I have some." I thought of my mother and my feelings about her, of which I had never spoken to anyone.

"Then there might be room for some of mine?" Oishi-sama mused, while glancing intently at me. I thought it best not to speak but nodded and waited for him to say more.

"I shall not be in need of many servants; I am not a man who asks for much. Soldiers, you know, have to be used to living rough, and a samurai is first and last and always a soldier." My master stopped and looked down intently upon the matted floor. "Still I shall need someone." He glanced at me and I bowed again. "A stupid servant may betray you without knowing how he did it, and the excuse that he did not mean to is of little comfort to the one who is betrayed. I need a servant who sees, who hears, but does not speak. Could you be such a servant, Jiro?"

"Oishi-sama, my tongue is not loose, I guard it. What my eyes see, my mouth shall not speak of." My master smiled. I was proud of my words for I thought they were well spoken.

"All servants are great gossips." I was about to protest but my master held up his hand. "You shall be no different, only I shall tell you what to say; I shall supply you with the gossip. You are a clever lad and sometimes you might make guesses at what I really mean. Those guesses you may keep to yourself. Trustworthy, yes, it is a splendid word, Jiro. Does that word fit you?"

"Oishi-sama, I shall do my best." I bowed until my head touched the floor. When I looked up again, to my surprise my master had drawn the smaller of his two swords. Its blade shone in the light of the little oil lamp that stood near. "It is sharp, Jiro, come nearer, feel it." I crawled on my knees toward my master and touched the steel with my hand.

"It is very sharp, Master," I said.

"It can rip open a belly or cut the throat of a traitor." Oishi-sama contemplated the blade. "Who knows what work it still needs to perform? Such secrets are locked in it." Then suddenly he turned its hilt toward me and said, "Put your hand on it, Jiro, and swear to be true."

"I shall be true and worthy of your trust," I said as my hand lightly touched the hilt of his sword.

"That will do, Jiro." Oishi-sama sheathed the sword once more. "A clever boy will think, and I cannot prevent you from that, only from telling your thoughts. It is late, go and sleep. The young need their sleep and their dreams; only we who are old dream best when we are awake." With a wave of his hand, as if he were shooing away a fly, he told me to leave. I crawled to the door and slid it open, then bowed once more, though I do not think my master saw it, and left.

I returned to the kitchen, but couldn't go to sleep. My mother was snoring. I went over to the alcove and looked at her. "Who was my father?" I asked in a low voice. "Was he a samurai?" To my disgust I wanted the answer to be yes, but there was no answer at all. My mother stuck her tongue out, licked her lips, and then turned over in her sleep. A little oil lamp was burning on the table where my mother prepared her vegetables. I blew it out, for oil is expensive and should not be wasted. The paper window shone brightly in the darkness. I went out into the courtyard, where the moon was almost full. "I have no one to talk to now except you, moon," I whispered. A little cloud raced past the lantern of the night, and for a moment the courtyard was in shadow. *From tomorrow everything will be different*, I thought, and then returned to the kitchen to try to get some sleep.

·4·

Oishi Chikara

I had expected everything to be altered from the next day, but nothing was. My master treated me as he had before, as if he did not remember, or chose not to recall, what had happened that night. Half out of pride, I, too, made sure that I acted in no way different from before. I said to myself, *What happened that night was merely a dream, so it didn't actually take place at all.* Naturally I knew that that was not true, for dreams are like the morning mist that disappears as soon as the sun rises, and I could recall every detail that had taken place that night.

"My father says that we are too few to hold the castle. So we shall make it ready for the Shogun's men and then we who are loyal shall commit seppuku." Oishi Chikara looked solemnly at me.

"I would not like to do that myself," I said, "and I do not see how that can help Lord Asano. It will make the Shogun angry, that is for sure."

"Only samurai can commit seppuku." Chikara looked at me with disgust. "Did you not know that? It will show our loyalty to our Lord."

I had not the least wish to slit open my belly, yet I could

not help but feel hurt at the thought that I wasn't allowed to. "But that will make certain that Lord Asano's brother will not be able to inherit the castle and become Lord of Ako." We were sitting outside, and the spring sun was warm. *Soon summer will be here and I shall go swimming*, I thought.

"If you and your father commit seppuku, what will happen to your mother and your sisters?" I asked.

"My uncle will take care of them," Chikara said lightheartedly. "But we shall not commit seppuku before it is certain that Lord Asano's brother will not be allowed to inherit the castle and become head of the clan. You see, if that happens, we will not be ronin."

Chikara is still a child, I thought, and then with a certain amount of pride I recalled that he was just two years older than I. It is because his mother and all the servants spoil him that he still is so childish. "And will the Shogun allow Lord Asano's brother to inherit the clan?" I asked.

"My father thinks not. There will be another meeting tonight; then he will suggest that we all commit seppuku."

"All of you?" I asked in amazement. The thought of so many samurai slitting open their bellies seemed almost ludicrous.

Chikara shook his head. "Only those of Lord Asano's retainers who are truly loyal will come tonight. If enough come then we will hold the castle against the Shogun's army. But my father thinks not many will come, maybe only a hundred."

"The people of the town hope you will give up the castle." It was rumored in town that Lord Asano's retainers had decided not to give up Ako castle, but vowed to defend it to the last man. The common citizens of the town were frightened, for if that was to happen they could lose their homes and maybe even their lives.

"Oh, they would not understand." Chikara shrugged his shoulders. "It is a matter of honor."

And we, we have no honor, I thought as I got up. "I must go and help my mother," I said. The cherry tree we had been sitting under had long lost its flowers, but some of the petals, all withered and yellow, still lay spread on the ground.

A little fewer than a hundred came to the meeting that night. Only about ninety of Lord Asano's samurai showed up, and the rest found somehow that they could not attend. Again I was to serve the tea if anyone should want it, outside in the castle yard, as no servants were allowed in the room where the meeting was taking place. I heard great shouts of approval at times, and some of the samurai who came out to get tea looked pleased, as if whatever decision had been made was one that they approved of. I knew I would learn what had happened from Chikara. I wondered if he spoke as freely to everyone as he did to me. The meeting broke up early; the moon had just risen when the last of the samurai left. Some of the young ones lived in the castle and others were on guard duty that night, but soon everything was quiet. I waited, half expecting and hoping that my master would send for me, but he didn't. I wished desperately that I had someone that I could talk to. I realized then that that was going to be the hardest part, not having someone to unburden oneself to. I could not talk freely to Chikara, he had too loose a tongue. Besides, he would be jealous if he knew I had his father's confidence. No, there was no one I could talk to, only my master and he had no wish to speak to me. *The moon,* I thought as I washed and put away the cups that had been used, *is a cold and distant friend to have.*

The next morning I learned what had been decided at the meeting the night before. The castle was to be surrendered to the Shogun's men, for ninety samurai, however brave they were, could not hold it. "We would run the risk of being laughed at," Chikara declared. I nodded my head in sympathy, for I knew that there was nothing a samurai feared more than being laughed at.

"Then you will all commit seppuku?" I asked innocently.

"No." Chikara shook his head. "My father has other plans."

I didn't ask what these plans were, for if I did not ask there was a better chance that I should learn what they consisted of. "When will the Shogun's soldiers come?" I asked instead.

"Soon. My father wants the castle cleaned and the streets and bridges in the town repaired. Then there is the matter of dividing up the clan money as soon as all Lord Asano's debts have been paid."

"The money, yes." I had heard Matsu talk about it. "Doesn't everything belong to the Shogun now?"

"The castle and any land that was Lord Asano's now belong to the Shogun. But a certain sum belongs to the clan, to all of us."

"What about the paper money that Lord Asano issued?

The Shogun won't honor that." I knew that was a real worry to many of the merchants and traders in the marketplace.

"My father will redeem it!" Chikara looked angrily at me. "Any such money will be changed into silver at sixty percent of its face value." Chikara looked as proud as if he himself had made the decision to redeem the clan's paper money.

"Some of the people in town feared that they could use that money to light their fires with. Sixty percent in silver will make them happy." I grinned. "I wish I had some myself."

"My father would wish the clan money to be divided equally among the retainers, but the others will not agree to that." Chikara looked very virtuous as he said this. He is not a very good-looking youngster; his eyes are very small and his figure already very squat. I am nearly as tall as he is, and my eyes are large and round.

"How much money is there?" I asked.

"That doesn't matter to you." Chikara had suddenly remembered that I was merely a poor servant boy and he the son of one of Lord Asano's chief retainers.

"You're right, it doesn't matter to me." I shrugged my shoulders to indicate that I didn't care either.

"My father says that there will be about six thousand ryo of silver to be divided," Chikara couldn't help saying.

"That is only thirty ryo to each," I pointed out. I had never held one ryo in my hand, yet I knew that thirty ryo was not a large sum to begin life as a ronin with.

"Some will get more than that and some less. But my father has savings."

"Will your father take service with some other Lord?" It was a question I very much wanted to know the answer to, for a servant follows his master.

"He could if he wanted to." Again Chikara recalled who he was and who I was. "My father could choose between any of the lords of Japan; they would all be eager to have him as their retainer." He glanced around and suddenly realized that he was standing in the kitchen. "He could even serve the Shogun if he cared to." Then he nodded haughtily to me and strutted from the room.

I looked at my mother, who was at her little table cutting up some cabbage. "Maybe you will end up making pickled cabbage for the Shogun, Mother," I said.

"Pickled cucumber is what he likes best," she said, putting down her knife.

"Who, the Shogun?" I asked.

"No, Oishi-sama, our master. He said I used too much salt. How can you pickle cucumbers without salt?" My mother looked angrily at me as if I was the one who had dared to find faults with her cucumber. "He is a fool," she added.

"Who," I asked, "our master, Chikara-san, or the Shogun?"

As a reply my mother only grunted, and she did not say another word until it was time for our supper. Then when I had already served our master, she suddenly said, "Maybe I meant you."

·5·

Okajima-sama

The fact that, in truth, all of Lord Asano's samurai were now merely ronin, that they no longer belonged in the castle or for that matter in the town, was obvious to everyone. The people of the town were in some ways more frightened of the samurai now than they had been before, for a ronin, a masterless samurai, is often not much better than a robber. If you are mistreated by a samurai, you can complain to his master; the samurai knows this and it curbs his arrogance. But a ronin has no master that you can complain to. You can appeal to his honor, but if he is hungry and cold, he probably is too poor to have any.

We, the servants of the samurai, felt the difference because few would sell us anything without being paid immediately. Credit is not easy for a ronin to get. It was known in the town that it was my master who stood for the distribution of the clan money, and most people thought Oishi-sama had made certain that his share would not be the smallest. Had the people of the town known that he had refused to take his share, but had given it to those of his fellow samurai who were poorest, they would not only have thought him a fool but also a bad risk to give credit to. As it was, I didn't have trouble buying what was necessary without paying, only promising that my master would pay soon.

"Who will be our master now?" the woman that I bought vegetables from asked.

"Who knows?" I shrugged my shoulders. "Maybe the Shogun will come himself," I suggested.

"Lord Asano was not a bad man." The woman paused and her forehead wrinkled in thought. Then she said, "He was a good master."

"Better than most and maybe better than what is coming," I said, wondering what the woman meant by "a good master." What would I mean myself by those words? My mother would think that a good master was one who was not stingy with the food and otherwise left you alone. I would say he was one who noticed the difference between you and his horse or his dog.

"It is better to be beaten by the stick you know than a stranger's," the woman muttered.

"That's true enough." I answered with a grin. There is so much more laughter in the country people than in the samurai, I thought. Yet their life is a hard one — if there is famine in the land it is they who die.

"Will Oishi-sama stay here?" she asked. When I didn't answer right away she added, "Maybe our new lord will keep him."

"He hasn't told me his plans, but as soon as he does I'll tell you." For a moment the woman thought I was serious, then she burst out laughing and I laughed too.

As I walked homeward one of Lord Asano's samurai came

storming by me, his largest sword drawn. The sunlight flashed in its blade. As he saw me he stopped, and for a moment I was frightened that he was going to test the sharpness of the blade by chopping off my head.

"Jiro!" he shouted so loudly that the whole town could have heard it. I bowed deeply and thought it best to fall on my knees.

"Yes, Okajima-sama," I said, bending my head once more.

"Tell your master that I have gone to chop off the head of that rat Ono." Okajima-sama stuck his sword back in its scabbard. "He has accused me of putting some of the clan money in my own sleeve." Okajima-sama was always a rather blustering sort of man, equally quick to anger and to laughter. I was surprised that he knew my name. Ono-sama was the leader of a group of Lord Asano's samurai who had refused to defend the castle against the Shogun's men. He and my master were not friends, but I knew from his servants that he was a difficult man to please.

"I shall tell him," I muttered and looked up at the samurai. He grunted and then walked off in the direction of that part of town where Ono-sama had his residence.

I got up and smiled at the thought of that fight. Ono was not the swordsman that Okajima was so it would not be a long battle, for it was certain that Okajima would win.

"Okajima-sama has asked me to tell you that he has gone to fight Ono-sama." I looked at my master. I had brought him tea and now thought it best to deliver the message.

"Why?" My master looked a little surprised. "Didn't he tell you? What did he say?"

"He said he was going to cut off the head of that rat Ono. He was so angry that he had already drawn his sword. Then he said that Ono-sama had accused him of stealing clan money." I was kneeling near the door of my master's room.

"I am sure he added no 'sama' to Ono's name. There is no man in Ako nor in all of Japan more honest than Okajima-Yasoemon. No wonder he is angry. He has been the treasurer of the clan for the last three years and Lord Asano trusted him more than he did himself." My master shook his head. "How foolish of Ono, for Okajima has another virtue which Ono does not possess: besides being honest he is one of our best swordsmen." My master waved me away.

I was just about to slide the door closed when my master called me back again. "Jiro, run along to the residence of Ono and see what has happened. If you see Okajima, tell him to come" — my master paused, then smiled as he said — "and drink a cup of sake with me."

I did not walk but obeyed my master by running to the house of the Ono family. As Ono had been one of Lord Asano's counselors, the house was grander than the surrounding ones. I could hear shouting from inside, and as the entrance gate was open I peeked inside. The servants of Ono-sama were arguing with Okajima-sama, who stood, sword drawn, on the threshold of the house. As the garden that surrounded the house was small, I could clearly hear every word that was spoken from where I stood. The servants kept telling the angry samurai that their master had suddenly taken ill and was asleep. I thought that Okajima-sama was making so much noise that no one in the whole town would be able to sleep for it. He was telling the servants his opinion of their master, which was not at all flattering. Finally he turned away, shouting over his shoulder, "Your master seems to fall very suddenly sick; tell him if he is well tomorrow I shall come and deliver him to a place where there is neither sickness nor health." He was storming out of the place when he spied me. "What are you doing here?" he shouted and pointed his sword at me.

"My master sent me," I replied, dropping to my knees. "He wanted to ask you to come —"

"Come!" Okajima-sama grumbled. "I am no dog anyone can shout for."

"To come and drink some sake with him," I hastily added, bobbing my head two or three times, hoping that I was not about to lose it.

"Sake!" Okajima laughed and put his sword back in its scabbard. "A word that has always been pleasing to my ear. Sake is a short sound but one full of meaning." His anger and fury were gone and as we walked back toward the castle together he talked to me, boasting about how much sake he could drink without getting drunk. *He is much like a child,* I thought, as I made noises of agreement to all he said, but I liked him. He walked fast and I had to half run to keep up with him. He noticed it and slackened his pace a little. "You are a good child," he said, as we entered the castle. "Remember to fill my cup to the brim." Then he laughed and slapped my back.

I went to the kitchen to get the cups and the sake. I knew that some of the other servants thought little of Okajima-sama because he cared so little about his dignity, but I liked him for it.

There were two sizes of pitcher for sake; I took the larger ones and filled them. Then I arranged some of the pickles my mother had made on two little plates, put all this on a tray together with two sake cups, and carried it up. The very animated conversation behind the door stopped as I paused before I slid it open. When I had finished serving them I kneeled and bowed to both of them. My master nodded to dismiss me, but suddenly turned to Okajima-sama and said, "I think I shall keep Jiro by me."

"Won't he talk?" Okajima looked me over as if the answer to his question could be read plainly from my appearance. "He must be as tightly sealed as a sake drum before it is opened."

"If he talks once he won't talk twice." My master Oishi-sama stared at me while he said this, and I looked back at him until he, not I, looked away. Then I bowed once more and crawled on my knees to the door. As I slid it closed I heard Okajima-sama say, "He is a little rascal, but I think he will do," then he laughed with that booming laughter of his. Down in the kitchen I thought of my master's words, "He won't talk twice." *Yes,* I thought, *if I betrayed him he would kill me, even if I had betrayed him inadvertently.*

·6·

The Last
Days in the Castle

The castle had never looked better in Lord Asano's time than now, when strangers would come to occupy it. It was as if my master's pride was involved — even the bridges and the roads in town had been repaired. The personal belongings of Lord Asano had been removed and sent to his wife's family, and as for the rest, a strict account had been made. Only a few days were left before the Shogun's officers would come to demand the castle. Rumor had been that retainers of Lord Asano were going to make a last stand inside its walls; therefore a small army was approaching the town of Ako. This pleased my master, for though he was going to hand over the castle peacefully, the more witnesses there were to the surrender, the more honorable he felt it would be. Two of the older samurai had been sent to the Shogun to plead that Lord Asano's brother might be allowed to become Daimyo of Ako and that the family name should not be removed from the list of the Lords of Japan.

"Tell your mother to clean the kitchen well." Oishi-sama looked around the room. I am sure he had never entered the place before; he didn't notice my mother, who was kneeling in a corner, her head bent.

"I shall, Master," I responded, bowing my head. I
spent the whole morning cleaning the kitchen.

"Tomorrow I shall go to meet the officers from the Sh
gun, and we shall hand over the castle in the morning
the following day. Whatever you have here that you ca
claim as yours or your mother's you must remove."

"We have but a bit of clothing and some bedding,"
said, bowing once more.

"Take it to my house tomorrow. Your mother can stay
there, but you must come back here. Tea might be
wanted." My master turned to leave, but in the doorway he
paused and said, "If there is hot water you may bring me a
cup now."

As our master left, my mother came to life. Grumbling
that she had two ears to hear with as well as a mouth for
speaking, she fanned the fire under the kettle. "But Oishi-
sama wanted to speak to a man," I said, grinning.

"Fools there are enough of. He needn't search for them
in my kitchen." My mother's vigorous fanning had made
the charcoal sprout little flames. "So back to the house it
is."

I shrugged my shoulders. I felt sorry for my mother, but
she could hardly expect to be handed over to the Shogun's
officers as a part of the castle. "I have been told that our
master has bought a house near Kyoto, and that we are to
go there as soon as the castle is no longer ours."

"Kyoto is very hot and there are no fish there," my
mother grumbled as she poured hot water into a little teapot.

"There is a river, I think, and there are many fine temples

and the Emperor's palace is there." I picked up the little tray my mother had prepared and started for the door. I liked the idea of going to Kyoto; it would be less boring than Ako.

"All places are the same," my mother muttered and then added, "but some are worse than others."

"Then they are not the same," I shouted at her as I left, but she had turned away.

"Jiro, we shall be moving to Kyoto as soon as the castle has been given back to the Shogun. I need a servant I can trust." My master sipped his tea but looked over the cup at me. I bowed but did not speak, for saying that I was such a servant, I thought, would be presumptuous.

"The loyalty of a vassal to his lord cannot be questioned, but a servant's loyalty is something else," Oishi-sama mused. I thought, *There are many stories of samurai who have proven traitors to their lords, surely my master would know them.* But I didn't allow my features to betray what I was thinking.

"Some of my servants I must dismiss, as there is no longer any lord paying me for my service. You and your mother are among those I shall keep." My master paused, and again I bowed but said nothing.

"I have spoken to you once before. Do you remember what I said?" My master put his teacup down on the table.

"I remember, Master, and I have spoken to no one, not even my mother. I can guard my tongue."

"I shall want you to wag it as well." Oishi-sama smiled. "I want you to keep your ears open and tell me what you

hear, for people will speak in front of you. What do they say in the town?"

"There is much talk and little sense to what most are saying. They feared that Lord Asano's men would fight, and that meant that their houses were in danger; they are glad that the castle is not to be defended. There is a great deal of laughter over the escape of Ono-sama. They say he left in the night and did not even take his granddaughter along, because he feared she would cry. When Okajima-sama came in the morning, the birds had flown and all that was left in the nest was the baby and its nurse." I allowed myself the slightest smile and my master laughed outright.

"Ono's courage was always located in his feet. I should have liked to have seen him fight Okajima." Oishi-sama shook his head. "Tell me everything you hear. Should anyone ask you about me, tell them that your master is retiring to Kyoto in order to grow flowers and study the teachings of Buddha."

"I will, Master." I was kneeling near the door, and I bowed my head down to the very floor.

"Remember that neither you nor your mother has ever felt hunger while in my house." My master was letting me know what I owed him and I could not help feeling hurt. But to a samurai we are not as they are. We are more like dogs that have to be taught respect with a stick.

"I shall always be loyal to you, Master," I said and bowed once more as deeply as before.

"You will and you shall. But guard your tongue concerning what you hear from me or my friends. If you should discover any secrets of mine, remember they become yours as well and they are to be kept well guarded even from your mother or any other servant of mine."

"I shall always obey you, Master," I mumbled, wondering if that was the right thing to say.

"Good." Oishi-sama drew a fan from his obi and with it pointed toward the door. I bowed a last time and then shuffled on my knees to the door and left.

As I made my way down to the kitchen I thought, *Yes, I will be loyal, but why?* I couldn't find any answer to that question.

Sometimes I think my mother is very clever and sometimes that she is stupid. When I returned to the kitchen she was drinking tea. She poured a cup for me as well. Then she said, "A samurai has a short memory when it comes to the likes of us, remember that, my boy. We play different games and so we have different rules." She sucked in her tea with a slubbering noise. "But they would like us to play according to their rules. A samurai's soul is mirrored in the blade of his sword, so they say, but we have no swords and therefore, in their opinion, we have no souls. When they deal with each other they are concerned with their honor, but when they deal with us they need not be." The last words were said with such bitterness that I thought, *She has been betrayed by one of them.* For a moment I smiled. This was the nearest my mother had ever come to telling me who my father was. I felt certain that he was a samurai.

My mother noticed my smile. "The pup born to a bitch is a dog, remember that! Don't go dreaming." She looked away and for a moment I could see that she might have been almost pretty when she was young. "I know they laugh at me, and that I am fat and ugly. They say I am lazy . . . and that is true too. I dreamed once and then . . . then I woke up. Don't dream . . . don't."

"My brother who died, did he have the same father as I?" It was a question I had often wanted to ask. Sometimes I thought of him, and what it would have been like to have had a brother.

"A dog does not know, or need to know, who is its father and neither do you." My mother looked angrily at me and I realized that it was a secret I probably would never learn from her. I growled like an angry dog and she laughed.

I cleaned the kitchen once more, until it was spotless. My mother did not help me but watched. My master did not desire food, for he had eaten at home, but in the evening I brought him sake as he was entertaining some friends. There was much talk of the past and a good deal of laughter as their spirits rose and the sake ebbed. The story of Okajima-sama's "fight" with Ono was told and retold several times. The hero was there in person. I liked him because he always said thank you to me when I poured him sake. Maybe I was but a dog to him, but then he was kind to dogs, and I was ever willing to wag my tail when shown kindness.

The Sword of Lord Asano

The last days before the surrender of the castle should have been days of shame and despair. Instead, they took on a festive air, as if it were New Year. A gaiety that was quite out of place for a group of people who in fact were masterless ronin spread among what was left of Lord Asano's retainers. A great deal of sake was drunk and old stories were told once more before they would be forgotten. Some of the retainers had left as soon as the clan money had been distributed. They were the ones who were eager to find a new lord to serve while they still had money in their purse. Some of them would be welcomed by other lords, but not all by far. A hundred years ago, when the lords of Japan were fighting like hungry dogs over bones to see who was to rule, any daimyo would be only too pleased to gather yet another samurai among his troops. But now after a century of peace under the Tokugawa shoguns, other things were valued more than the skill of a swordsman.

My master could easily have found a lord who would be eager to employ him, for he had been in charge of Ako castle for many years and knew how to manage men and property. It was the younger samurai who would find it most difficult to obtain new positions. Once their money had been spent, they would be forced by the hunger in their stomachs to take up mean crafts in order to survive. Some might be lucky enough to find a rich merchant who had a daughter and ambitions for his grandchildren to rise in the world, and therefore would like a son-in-law who wore the two swords. But in order to achieve this it was important not to be too impoverished. A samurai who had hidden his swords out of shame, and had become a mender of broken umbrellas, might not look very attractive in the eyes of a wealthy merchant or his daughter. No, the future of Lord Asano's retainers was not as bright and sunny as the days were while we waited for the Shogun's delegates to arrive.

My master, together with the more important retainers of Lord Asano, had gone to meet the Shogun's officers and pay his respects to them as they entered the Ako territory. Oishi-sama wanted to do everything as correctly as possible. He wanted the reputation of the retainers of Lord Asano to be spotless. In Edo the shogunate had been worried that Lord Asano's samurai would defend the castle and stand a siege. So though they had sent only fifty soldiers to act as guards for the officials who were to take charge of the castle, they had asked the neighboring lords to send troops, should it be necessary to use force. These troops were now marching toward Ako and were scheduled to arrive at the same time as the Shogun's party.

All this pleased my master for he wanted the takeover of the castle to be a memorable event that would not soon be forgotten. The Shogun's deputies were to be housed in an inn in Ako for their first night in the city, then on the following morning the castle would be officially turned over to them. But before that Oishi-sama wished them to come to the castle and inspect the papers and accounts of the castle, as well as the building itself, so that in the morning this would not be necessary.

The day before Lord Asano's retainers relinquished the castle, the little town of Ako was filled with soldiers. The neighboring lords had sent their very best troops, and their officers were dressed in the most splendid armor. The Shogun's soldiers had taken over the little inn, making it the residence, for the moment, of the officials they were escorting.

I was certainly the fly on the wall that day, but some of the events that I describe now I was told about much later. The two officers of the Shogun came in the afternoon to go through papers and accounts. They were men in their best age, neither young nor old but at midtide in their life. The big gate to the castle had been thrown open and Oishi-sama met them at the threshold. Both sides bowed deeply to each other and then my master spoke.

"According to the will of the Shogun Tokugawa Tsunayoshi, I am to deliver the castle of my Lord Asano-sama into your hands. I wish you to inspect the papers and accounts concerning the domain which my master Lord Asano ruled. Please follow me." He led the Shogun's men to the room where the castle accounts and other papers were kept. The officers gave but a cursory glance at them and said they were satisfied that they were in order. Then Oishi-sama led them on an inspection tour of the castle. At different points guards were posted who saluted them as they passed. At last he took them to the main room. My master had been accompanied by his two friends Yoshida and Hara-sama. Now all seated themselves. The Shogun's officers complimented my master upon the condition of the castle and indeed what they had seen of the town of Ako as well. My master said he had not had much time to do all that he had wished to do, but he was thankful that they had looked at everything with kind and not critical eyes. Then he took out a piece of paper, a petition to the Shogun, and read it aloud. "We shall tomorrow morning as the sun rises deliver to you this castle as ordered by the Shogunate. Our Lord being dead and our clan abolished, we are but the shadows of the men we once were, living as we do in the midst of such an overwhelming calamity. It is only because it is our hope that our Lord's brother, Daigaku, might be allowed to inherit the house, that we are still alive in the midst of our shame. It is well known that the first ancestors of the Asano house were under the special patronage of the Shogun Tokugawa Ieyasu, and his line has enjoyed for a century an honorable position among the lords of our country. Our hearts are bursting with grief to see it become extinct. Our earnest supplication at this juncture is that, as a special favor, Daigaku be appointed successor in whatever way the Shogun deems fit. Should this petition not be granted, then we shall kill ourselves before the grave of our lord and thus discharge our duty as retainers. If you have any sympathy for us, we sincerely beg of you to hand this petition to the government and use your influence with the Shogun and the Councilors on our behalf."

The two officers did not answer. They only nodded to

indicate that they had understood, but they took the petition with them as they left.

"Is there still sake left?" my master asked as he and his friends returned.

"Enough to fill a bath," I said and made ready to fetch some.

"That would be something," Hara-sama said with a grimace. "One would empty the bath by drinking it."

"In the winter," Yoshida-sama joined in, "I like to have a cup of warm sake while I take my bath. It is marvelous to sit and sip it, warm inside and outside."

I brought the sake and the last of the pickles my mother had made, but when I returned the mood of my master and guests had changed.

"You cannot live in the same world with your lord's murderer," I heard Oishi-sama say just as I entered.

"That is true." Hara-sama nodded, but looked at me as I brought the sake.

"Yet we must wait, for Kira will be well guarded, and he will expect us to avenge the death of Lord Asano." Yoshida-sama sighed. "I fear that I shall be too old and too feeble, if I live, to wield a sword."

"You shall live to see Kira's head placed on the tomb of our lord. For an old man you are young yet. Here, I want to show you something." From a bundle lying near him Oishi-sama took a sword. He carefully drew it from its scabbard. The blade shone bright. "This is Lord Asano's sword, the one he drew in the Shogun's palace. His wife has sent it to me, for the soul of our lord will find no peace until we have avenged him. Once it only grazed Kira; next time it shall end his life." My master carefully sheathed it again and tucked it out of sight in the bundle. "Once," he began, smiling, "long ago there was a man named Minamoto Hiromasa. He was of the imperial family, his grandfather being Emperor Daigo. Hiromasa was a skillful musician who played the lute well. He wanted to improve himself and therefore asked the famous lute player Semimaru to become his teacher. But Semimaru refused to take the prince as a pupil, and for three years every evening Hiromasa waited outside the door of the musician, asking to be let in. At last such perseverance could not but impress Semimaru, and he allowed Hiromasa to become his pupil. We are not asking to learn to play the lute, but we shall have the same patience as Minamoto Hiromasa had, and the gods shall reward it as well."

For a moment every one of them was silent. Then they all took their sake cups and lifted them in a salute to each other. I, the fly on the wall, had been kneeling by the door. Now I quietly slid it open and left.

·8·

The Surrender
of the Castle

I think there were few, if any, of the samurai in the castle who slept that night. I followed my master around silent as a shadow. I think he was aware that I was there, and he didn't mind it. Maybe I was not so much a shadow as the dog that follows at his master's heel. In the early morning before sunrise he mounted the tower near the gate. From there you can see far and wide. Smoke was rising from the camps of the troops on the outskirts of town. They were getting ready to take part in the final surrender of our castle. Nearly all the retainers of Lord Asano were in the castle that night, all of them dressed either in armor or in the best clothes they possessed. The sky was turning pink. Soon the sun would be rising and then . . .

"Did you take everything out of the kitchen that belonged to you?"

"Yes, Master," I whispered, "also some of the cups that are yours."

"Good." Oishi-sama nodded. "I was about your age when my father took service with Lord Asano; soon there will be more white hair than black on my head. Ako is a good place to live; I never thought that I should leave it. Men are like dead leaves, that the winds can play with and deposit where they choose. Listen!" Faintly I could hear a conchshell trumpet that was being blown in one of the camps. "As the sun rises we shall open the gates wide, for those who have come to take our home and our honor; then we shall leave and never enter its portals again." For a moment Oishi-sama stayed, looking for the last time around the land he loved, pausing as he looked toward the sea where several ships that had brought troops lay at anchor. He smiled at the sight, then climbed down the stairs to give the order for the main gate to be thrown open.

Just at sunrise the troops led by the Shogun's officers entered the castle, the exchange of the guards was made, and then Oishi-sama led the soldiers of his lord for the last time from the castle. I — the dog, the shadow, the fly on the wall — followed a few paces behind them. I wondered if my master had not sent my mother home just because he feared that she would have joined in the parade, making it look ridiculous. She might even have told the Shogun's troops what she thought of them. As it was now, the troops that had come to garrison the castle seemed deeply touched by the sight of the samurai marching to their fate as ronin.

My master led them to Kegakuji temple, where the graves of Lord Asano's parents were. There he reported what had happened to his lord's ancestors, retelling the fate of Lord Asano. It was but a short speech, and when he had finished that sad tale he said, "Now it is up to yourselves if you still wish to pay your allegiance to that lord, who while he lived served you well. Some people may call us ronin, masterless; I prefer to say that I am still a loyal retainer of

Lord Asano. We all owe debts; those that can be paid in money are the least important. Until that debt I owe my Lord is paid I shall never feel free."

Most of Lord Asano's retainers shouted their agreement, but some kept silent. They had marched to the temple together, but they left it drifting in small groups or alone, each man wondering what to do now and what his fate would be.

"I shall go to Edo," Okajima-sama declared; he was walking beside my master.

"At present Kyoto suits me better. Some relatives have taken a house for me in the small village near it," my master replied. "But Edo will be fine . . . it is the dohyo," he added and smiled. The dohyo is the ring where the wrestlers fight. Kira, the enemy who had caused the downfall of Lord Asano, lived in Edo, the Shogun's town. If Asano's retainers were to revenge themselves it would have to be done in Edo.

Okajima-sama laughed and repeated my master's words, "The dohyo."

I was surprised that my master did not invite Okajima-sama inside when they came to his house. But they parted at the gate, with much bowing and wishing of luck to each other. As I entered the courtyard I understood suddenly why my master did not want company. In the little courtyard in front of the house, under a cherry tree there was a bench, where Oishi-sama had seated himself. He was breathing hard and I noticed little pearls of sweat on his forehead. "I am not feeling well, Jiro," he said as I came up to him. "I shall sit for a while until I catch my breath again."

I didn't know what I was supposed to do, go inside or stay. My master pointed to the ground near him and I sat down, waiting for him to speak.

"You must be my eyes, my ears, Jiro, and maybe my mouth as well. They will come spying here and in Kyoto as well. Tell me all you hear and if they approach you . . . which they probably will, then —"

"I shall tell them nothing!" I burst out. "I am not for sale."

"Oh, but I want you to be." My master smiled. "Tell them that you do not care for me, but don't be too willing, don't make it too easy or they may suspect a trap. Be greedy for the money they offer, I shall tell you what you are to tell them. It may not happen here but maybe later in Kyoto, if someone should approach you within the next few days, then you can tell them the truth, that I am not feeling well at all. You can tell them that I have . . . a fever and that" — my master got up — "I have gone to lie down in my room."

The next day my master was much worse; he did not eat anything at all, only drank a little tea. I waited upon him, spending most of the day kneeling silently in a corner of his room. Everyone was as quiet as mice; a doctor was called, of whom it was said that he knew all the medicines of China. He had a white beard and looked very wise. He shook his head several times, and then he ordered my master to take twice daily a very bitter medicine, which he declared was so precious that it could cure nearly anything. But it certainly did not help my master, for he got sicker and sicker. Once more the doctor was sent for. He frowned when he saw his patient and prescribed another potion; this one was green and he said it was much stronger. It may have been and Oishi-sama took it, but he only grew weaker and weaker.

My master would moan in his sleep and when he woke he would say things that made no sense. He did not seem to recognize anyone who came into the room, and his fever rose and rose. I was ordered to stay with him, and I even took my bedding and slept in a corner of his room. An old woman helped me do the nursing; she had been with the family so long that she could tell stories of my master when he was a child, and she claimed that she had carried him on her back when he was a baby. Oishi-sama's wife came often; she was a very silent woman and one never knew what she was thinking. I do not know if she liked me, and I am certain that she did not care for my mother.

Sometimes I thought that time moved so slowly, while I knelt in my corner, that it might even have stopped. Especially at night I felt like that, and if it had stopped, then the darkness would last forever. I thought a great deal about what had happened and what was going to happen. My master's plan, I knew by now, was to avenge Lord Asano by killing the man who had insulted his master. A little over sixty of Lord Asano's retainers had made a solemn agreement to do this deed and had signed it with their blood.

If they succeeded in killing Kira, then they in turn would be killed, that was certain. At best they would be allowed to commit seppuku; the worst would be a death on the execution grounds with their heads exhibited afterward on stakes. Many of them had wives and children. What would happen to them? How could it help Lord Asano's spirit? But maybe it could not rest in its grave until it was avenged. But did it matter? Well, I was not a samurai so maybe I just did not understand it; that is what my master's son Chikara would have said. *It's funny,* I thought, *they have a lot to lose and I have so little, yet I don't want to die and they do.* These were some of the thoughts I had while waiting on my master through his sickness.

Suddenly one morning, I woke hearing my master's voice. He was not raving, uttering words meaningful only to himself, but was demanding a cup of tea.

"How many days have passed?" he asked, and when I told him he said, "My soul, I think, went traveling without taking my body along."

The doctor came and declared that he had cured the patient. He was given a drink of sake and a gift. He left some more medicine for my master, who never took it.

·9·

The Samurai Spy

My master got better very slowly; he was still extremely weak and therefore it would be some time before he was well enough for us to move to Kyoto. I still waited upon him; it was as if some unspoken agreement had been made that I was to be his personal servant. My poor mother was again the lowest among the women in the kitchen, fetching water and doing all the heavy work. My master would send me out into the town, to gather what he called "news." I would return telling him what little I had found out. But one day what he had foretold happened.

I had gone down to the shore because I liked to watch the fishermen bringing in their catch. I was thinking that I would like to be a fisherman; it seemed to me a good life, especially if you had your own little boat. I was standing, dreaming, when all of a sudden I felt a hand on my shoulder. I turned to look into the face of a samurai. I immediately fell to my knee; it is always safest to do that, for a samurai can kill you and need only protest that you had been behaving insultingly, to get away with your murder.

"Are you a servant to Oishi Kuranosuke?" he asked and

smiled, but the smile did not fit his face, it made his features look like a mask.

"Yes, master," I said and bowed my head.

"How is he? And what does he do?" As I didn't answer right away he added, "I am an old friend of his."

"He has been very sick," I said.

"But he is better now?" The samurai had stopped smiling and was looking down upon me as if I were a bit of dirt.

"Oh, much better, but still very weak; he only sits under the cherry tree in the garden."

The samurai grunted, and then with his finger he beckoned for me to get up. "I hope he will revenge his master soon and kill that dog Kira."

"Oh, I know nothing of that," I said as I rose and tried to look bewildered, as if I had not understood what had been said.

"Kuranosuke is a sly one, what goes on in his head does not show on his face," the samurai grumbled. "I would like to be in on the revenge; after all, I have served Lord Asano as well."

If he had been one of Lord Asano's retainers I had never seen him before. I was beginning to enjoy the game. "Please, sir," I said, "why don't you come and visit my master? I am sure he would like to see you."

"Maybe I shall." The samurai looked as if he had run out of words. He was probably better at wielding his sword than his tongue.

"Shall I tell him you will call?" I asked.

"Yes . . . yes, I will call on him . . . soon." With those

words the samurai turned on his heels and walked away, giving me no name to tell my master.

I almost laughed; as a spy the samurai was a failure. I guessed that he was a low retainer of some daimyo and that he had been sent to try and find out what my master's plans were. Well, he had found out nothing but that my master had been sick and was still weak but recovering. That news he was welcome to.

I was eager to tell what had happened to me, but Chikara met me at the entrance to the house, with the words, "My father is sleeping." I knew he was very jealous of the close relationship that had developed between his father and me, so I merely bowed, and said nothing, trying to look as humble as possible.

"You can rake the front here," he said and pointed to the little yard between the gate and the house itself. I bowed once again and went to fetch a bamboo rake. I was carefully raking the few leaves together when I heard my master calling "Jiro." When I turned, he was standing in the doorway, looking very annoyed.

"I was told that you were sleeping and did not wish to be disturbed," I said, on purpose not mentioning who had been doing the telling.

"When you have been in town I wish you to report back to me; should I be sleeping, then you can wait in the room until I wake. Put that rake away and come inside and tell me what you have heard." Oishi-sama turned, and as he went back inside I couldn't help noticing that he did not stand as straight as he used to.

After I put the rake away, I went to my master's room;

his bedding was disturbed so I could see he had been sleeping. He said, "You can bring me some tea later, but first tell me what you have heard in town."

"A samurai stopped me to ask about your health, claiming he was one of Lord Asano's retainers. He said he wanted to know when you were going to avenge your lord, and he said he would like to join in the venture."

"And did you believe him?" Oishi-sama frowned.

I shook my head. "I have never seen him before; I think he was new in Ako and he spoke more as if he came from the east or maybe even from the north. He had a beard and a scar on his left cheek."

"He was sent here to check on me, I am sure. What did you tell him?"

"That you had been ill and were recovering but were very weak still. When he asked if, and when, you were to avenge your lord, I said I knew nothing of that. He looked as if he did not care for the work he had been given." I didn't want to tell my master that I had thought the man a fool, for even though he probably was an enemy of my master he was still a samurai and as such an equal, while I was only a fly on the wall.

"Very good." My master smiled. "If he comes to talk to you again try to find out where he comes from. Tell him, too, that we are shortly moving to Kyoto, and that I have rented a house near that town. You can tell him I am busy reading the lotus sutra and I am eager to plant some trees before I die. If he believes it, well and good, and if he doesn't . . . well and good as well. Now you can bring me some tea."

I brought the tea. My master was now in a very good humor; it was as if what I had told him pleased rather than frightened him. The fact that what he had been expecting had happened seemed to him a good omen. That night, as he went to sleep, his last words to me were, "If they offer you money, Jiro, take it." Then he laughed and said, "But don't sell me too cheaply."

I met the samurai once more while we lived in Ako. It was at night and my master had sent me to purchase some sake. Friends of his had arrived and our house had turned out to be as dry as a river in the summer. I just came from the sake shop carrying two bottles, and by the looks of him I should think the samurai too was carrying a couple of bottles of sake, but his were inside him. At first he did not recognize me, but then unfortunately he did and hollered "wait" at my back. I thought first of running; I could easily have outrun him, but then I thought better of it and waited.

"You little Oishi bedbug, are you not well enough brought up to bow to your betters?" The samurai swayed back and forth, but did not tumble. "You can tell your master that the nail that raises its head is hammered down." Then he laughed. "That, you little cockroach, is a proverb your master can contemplate."

"I shall tell it to my master; I am sure he will be grateful." I bowed my head, then suddenly I had a good idea and said, "But won't you come back with me? My master is having a few friends in for some sake. I am sure he will be pleased to see you."

"Some other time I will come to see your master, but not to drink sake." At his last words he laughed as if it was a joke which he found extremely funny. I was just about to do some more bowing prior to leaving when he stopped me by raising his hand.

"Tell him, you ill-bred cockroach, another proverb: to kill a general, first shoot his horse." Again he shook with laughter over his own wit. Then, well satisfied with himself, he strutted off down the street. I watched him until I saw him enter a little sake booth, then I hurried home, carrying both sake and news.

As I poured sake for my master and his friends, two Asano samurai, I wondered if I should tell what had happened to me now or wait until they had gone. But Oishi-sama guessed from the expression on my face that I was carrying some news that I was bursting to tell and he asked me what had happened.

"I met the samurai, Master, the one who spoke to me before," I said and looked down at the matted floor, thus giving my master the choice of when he wanted to hear it.

"Yes, and what did he want?" My master smiled and told his friends of my previous meeting.

"He was filled with sake, and when he left me he went to get more. He wanted to give you advice, what he meant by that I didn't understand." Then I told the two proverbs the samurai had spoken, and also that he had said that he would come for a visit someday but not to drink sake.

"I think it must have been one of Kira's retainers," one of the samurai said.

"I think he is more likely to be a retainer of Lord Uesugi of Yonezawa, for that daimyo is in truth a son of Kira's who was adopted by the Uesugi family, to which Kira's wife is related. They are well known for having among their samurai the best archers of Japan. Did you say anything to him?" my master asked, turning to me.

"I asked him to return with me to drink some sake, I said that I was sure you would welcome him. It was then that he said that someday he would come but not to drink sake." I noticed that the two samurai had emptied their sake cups so I refilled them. "Was that wrong?" I asked, looking at my master.

"No, you have done well." Oishi-sama turned to the others and said, "We must have patience. If we attacked Kira now when he expects it and is prepared for it, we would fail."

·10·

We Move to Yamashina

Finally we moved, not to Kyoto but to a small village between Lake Biwa and Kyoto. The house my master had bought was more splendid than one would expect a ronin to own. It was situated on the hillside above the village. From its garden you had a view of the road that leads from Edo, where the Shogun lives, to Kyoto, where the palace of the Emperor is. Above the house was a temple, and we could hear the chanting of the priests and monks when they said their prayers.

I was a little disappointed, for I had hoped that we would live in the middle of the town, not an hour's walk from it. To fool his enemies my master affected the life of a man retired from the bustle of the world. He even transferred the headship of the family to his son. Chikara grew at least five inches in his own esteem because of this. My master also rented a small pavilion in the grounds of a temple in Kyoto. The temple had some connection to the Asano family; my master had a tomb erected in its garden to his master. In it was buried the kimono of state of Lord Asano.

The second night we were in our new home, my master called me. He was alone and I knelt just inside the door. It was a warm summer evening. My master had been fanning himself, and now he closed the fan and pointed with it to a place in front of him. I scurried across the matted floor and kneeling, bowed to him.

"Jiro, your master has given up all hope of avenging his Lord. He is busy tending flowers and studying the lotus sutra. Since his illness he has grown old and weak, he is more concerned about the next world than this one." I looked surprised for I thought that my master had recovered very well; then, judging from the expression on his face, I realized what he meant.

"I understand, Oishi-sama," I said.

"At present Kira is well protected. We must make him feel safe and secure, so that he will no longer be on his guard. For that we need patience, and the young are not patient." My master frowned and mumbled to himself. "If the nightingale doesn't sing, I shall wait until it sings." Then smiling a little, as if what he had said had given him pleasure, he looked at me. "We should be like Tokugawa Ieyasu; he had patience and that won him all of Japan . . . Now what are you going to say, if someone asks you how your master is faring?"

"I will say" — I paused a moment, not sure of what I would say, or dared tell my master, then I made up my mind — "I shall tell anyone who asks that my master's sword has grown rusty and that he cares for nothing but the flowers that grow in his garden, and like most old men he resembles a child." I watched the expression on my master's face as I spoke. When I said that his sword had grown rusty he made a grimace, but as I finished he laughed.

"That will do, you little imp. But don't overdo it; first

be loyal, for only a fool gives away the wares he has come to market to sell. If you can, try to remember what those who ask look like, and guess where they come from." My master raised his fan, pointing to the door with it. I bowed my head until my forehead touched the tatami and left, bowing once more as I slid the door closed.

The very next day I was stopped by a young samurai in the road not far from the house. He asked first the distance to Kyoto and, when I answered, made some comments upon the summer weather. I knew immediately that he was a spy sent from Kira, for no samurai would converse with a servant boy about the state of the weather. I agreed that it was hot and told him that Kyoto would be even hotter, for in Yamashina you sometimes got the breeze blowing from the lake.

"Who is your master?" the samurai finally asked.

"Oishi-sama," I answered. I had been kneeling all the time.

"Oishi!" The samurai screwed up his face. "Was he not one of Lord Asano's men?" I nodded but said nothing.

"Very unfortunate affair." The samurai looked for a moment appropriately sad.

"It must have been very hard for your master to see his Lord being forced to commit seppuku and his clan dispersed." Again I nodded rather than saying anything; after all, it was a statement I could hardly help agreeing with. "So what is he doing now?" As this was a question which could not be answered with a nod, I said, "My master is growing peonies, they are a flower which he is fond of."

"Ah!" This time it was the samurai that nodded. "Peonies . . . I prefer chrysanthemums myself."

"He is also studying the sutras. He has grown very old since Lord Asano died." The last I said with a slight tone of disgust, pretending a contempt which I did not feel.

"I must be on my way. When next I come I shall pay my respects to your master. Here!" He threw a copper coin in the dirt, I bowed and muttered thanks. The samurai did not wait to hear it, but stalked away as if he suddenly felt that he had wasted enough time on me. I put the coin in my sleeve and then went home to recount the incident to my master.

"He said he would come to visit me." Oishi-sama smiled. "He is either one of Kira's men or of Lord Uesugi's. If you see him again, tell me even if he does not speak to you."

A few days later an incident happened that nearly caused my mother to be dismissed. Officially my master had retired and his son Chikara was now the head of the house. But no one took this very seriously except for Chikara and his mother. She, being very fond of her son, rejoiced at his advancement and would kneel and bow to him as deeply as she did to her husband. Chikara enjoyed this, especially when it was accompanied with little gifts, as it often was. Chikara had a sweet tooth and liked bean-paste cakes. Having received two cakes from his mother, he ate one but hid the other to be eaten later. Unfortunately my mother found his hiding place and being as fond as he was of bean-paste cakes, and much less used to getting them, she ate it. Chikara, who seldom laughed and never at himself, made much of it. A cake belonging to the head of the house had mysteriously vanished! My master's wife solved the mystery by slapping my mother's face twice. My mother, who had at first declared herself innocent, then prostrated herself upon the floor and confessed to her crime. It was all more ridiculous than anything else.

My mother was dragged in front of Oishi-sama for judgment. She lay pitifully sobbing on the floor awaiting her sentence, while mother and son told of her crime. I was listening outside the door, feeling sorry for my mother, for I knew that she feared being sent away to the country, where she would be set to work in the fields. I heard her declare between sighs and sobs that she would never do such a thing again, but work even harder than she had before. (The latter was not such a difficult promise to make as she was very lazy.) The end of the affair was that she got some strokes with a bamboo stick and was allowed to stay. As head of the servants, it was Matsu who beat her. I asked her if it had hurt, but she only grinned and didn't reply. *Sooner or later,* I thought to myself, *you are going to end up in the rice paddies.*

My master had ordered some changes to be made in the house, and we had a group of carpenters working, building a small addition to the house. I liked to watch them; I envied them their skill and thought that someday I might like to become a carpenter myself. Because I had been watching them, I noticed immediately when a newcomer joined their band. He helped by handing the workmen their tools or holding a piece of wood for them while they cut it. He was a grown man, doing a boy's work. He would sit apart when the others ate their rice balls for lunch; he tried to talk to the maids, and to my mother as well. When I asked my mother what he had said to her, she shrugged her shoulders and replied that it was nothing of any importance.

I told her that it was, and she finally confessed that he had asked where Oishi-sama slept. "I told him," she said, "that he slept in the big room, and that he always kept his sword right beside him in case a robber came. He is no carpenter. If he had to use a hammer he would hit his fingers with it." She laughed.

I went immediately to my master and told him about the new workman and that I thought he was another spy. I told it as if it was my mother who had discovered the intruder, thinking that it might do her reputation some good with my master.

He declared that she ought to be rewarded with a bean cake, but I am not sure he believed me. That evening he called the head carpenter into his room and asked him when his work would be finished. The carpenter appeared very nervous, and when my master asked who the newcomer was that he had noticed that morning, his face grew red. He declared as he blushed that it was his wife's brother who had merely come for a visit, and he had taken him along to help as he was poor and needed work. But he was not worth his pay so he would dismiss him.

"No, no, not for my sake. It could make trouble in your family; after all, your wife's brother is not a stranger in the house," my master declared. "I had just noticed him and thought that he might be from Yonezawa or from Edo." The carpenter replied that his wife was from the town of Osaka and that his brother-in-law lived there.

Oishi-sama smiled and said it was of no importance, but next day when the carpenters came the "brother-in-law" was not among them.

·11·

Goro

On the fourteenth of each month, my master had asked the samurai who lived in or near Kyoto to come to Reikon temple. Ostensibly this was to pray for their master's soul at the grave wherein my master had buried Lord Asano's kimono. This I think was merely an excuse for the meeting. The spirit of revenge had to be kept burning, and at such meetings an ember could be fanned into flame. Also it was important for Oishi-sama to keep control over the younger samurai and prevent them from doing anything foolish. Some of the young men had received so little of the clan money that they were already destitute, and they had to be helped.

On these visits I would accompany my master. I would cook his meals in the temple kitchen and serve him in the room he had rented. He had asked as many as possible to attend on the fourteenth day of the eighth month, as he had news for them. We left the day before and arrived so late at the temple that my master declared that there was no need for me to cook, as he would go straight to sleep after he had prayed at the tomb. I laid out his bedding, and I would sleep outside the door to his room, so that he easily could call me should he need me. Men long past their youth, like my master, do not feel hunger as the young do. I watched Oishi-sama enter his room, and then I went in search of something to eat. In the kitchen I discovered a young acolyte devouring rice as if he had not eaten in a week. He was a boy my own age or possibly a year or two older. He had just filled his bowl from a pot that stood beside him. I looked into it and saw there were at least two bowlfuls left.

"Charity," I said, "is a sign of holiness and it is said that Buddha himself would rather watch a starving man fill his belly than eat himself. Now if you would give me the rice left in that pot, you would be one step nearer to becoming a Buddha."

The boy, a sour-looking child, gave a grunt and picked up the last of the rice in his bowl with his chopsticks. Then he made a face not altogether respectful at me, and started to fill his bowl again from the pot. As he dished the last bit of rice into it I took the bowl from him and with many words of thanks started to pop the rice into my own mouth with my fingers, since I had no chopsticks. The boy reached for the bowl, but I jumped out of his way and did not return it to him before I had finished.

"Delicious," I cried and bowed mockingly. I thought for a moment that he would fight, but instead he asked if I had come with the samurai, and if I was his servant.

"No, no," I declared, "he is my servant. I am actually an agent of the Shogun, who has come to inspect the state of affairs in Kyoto." I put on an air of great importance which made the youngster laugh.

"And how do you find them?" he asked.

"The portions of rice are too small," I said. "Except for that, things are not altogether bad." I sat down near him and asked, "What's your name? Mine is Jiro."

"Goro, and that's why I am here. I have four brothers and all of them nearly as hungry as I was. The oldest is staying at home, being spoiled by my mother. The next one was the lucky one. He was adopted by a rich merchant in Osaka who had no son of his own. As for the other two, they may have become beggars for all I know or care."

"I had one brother. He died before he was introduced to me, or if he was I don't remember it, for I was only one year old then. I hope he was lucky when he was reborn, but I'm not too sure, for bad luck seems to run in our family. He was probably reborn a river rat . . . Do they feed you well in the temple?" I asked.

"Fish, shrimps, squid, or anything you care to have and as much as your belly can hold. The truth is that the priest who is in charge is as mean as can be; grass doesn't grow where his foot has trodden. He believes we can live on prayers and air. I shall probably get a beating for having eaten this pot of rice, but it was worth it." Goro slapped his stomach. "Let's share the rest of it," he said and divided what was left in the pot into two portions. My share was a good-sized rice ball.

"When your belly is full you can face anything, even a bamboo cane." Goro laughed. "Besides, it's so much easier to say your prayers when you're not hungry. Does your master beat you?"

"No, he never has." I suddenly realized that I was lucky in having Oishi-sama as my master.

"If he ever does, remember to scream as loudly as you can, even if it doesn't hurt. That's the surest way to make them stop."

"I shall," I said, wondering if that was true of my master. I felt that Oishi-sama would just have contempt for the youngster who screamed and might even hit him harder. *He would never hit me because that was beneath his dignity, but he might kill me,* I thought.

"I think I shall run away soon," Goro confessed. "Next spring I shall go to Osaka. People are so rich there that they wouldn't bend down to pick up a copper coin lying in the street."

"How did they get so rich? Are they all samurai?" I asked.

"Samurai!" Goro said with disgust. "No, they're merchants, selling things. It might have been great once to be a samurai but that's all over now."

"Merchants can't wear the two swords," I said with equal disgust. After all, my master was a samurai.

"In Osaka there are many traders who have samurai working for them. They hide their swords, being ashamed, and then load ships or do anything at all for a few coppers," Goro said and sneered.

"I heard someone say that there has been peace too long and everyone is growing soft. He said you could get further knowing how to conduct the tea ceremony or arranging flowers than by being skillful with your sword." This was something I had heard an old samurai say to my master. He was a close friend of Oishi-sama. His name was Hara Soemon and he was living in Osaka.

"Yes, they would like to go hunting for heads again."
Goro grinned. "But that is all over; we get more silver from
merchants than we get from your precious samurai. It's as
difficult to wring a copper coin out of them as to wring
water from a stone."

"Is that what your priest is saying?" I suddenly realized
that both Goro and I were just repeating words we had
heard from our masters.

Goro nodded. "But it's true that in Osaka there is money
to be earned, especially if you're not too particular in how
it's earned."

I wondered what Goro meant by that. Was he thinking
of stealing? I had heard of bands of robbers that used youngsters. It was probably just talk. It was true that some merchants had grown very rich, but after all what were they? A
samurai could kill a merchant and go free if he could prove
that the merchant had not treated him with the respect he
deserved. Why, a merchant was ranked below a farmer, and
what were farmers but clods working in the rice paddies? I
rose to go, thanking Goro for the rice; I wanted to keep
him as a friend as he would be useful whenever we stayed
in the temple.

The moon, the lantern of the night, was bright and full.
I sat for a while in the garden by the tiny pond where a few
fat carp swam. In the bushes fireflies were playing. I tried
to count them but there were too many. Maybe someday I
would run away too, to Osaka or Edo. But for the time
being I would stay, not so much because I felt loyal to my
master but because I was curious about what would happen.
It was like a story; I had heard the beginning, and now I

would like to stay to hear the end as well. A bat swooped so near me that I could feel a little puff of wind from its wings. *How strange to live by night,* I thought, *and sleep during the day.* I picked up a little stone and threw it into the pond; so still was the night that the plop, as the stone hit the water, was so loud that I almost feared it could wake my master.

·12·

I Am Wounded

I woke very early because of a pigeon that had come to
investigate what was lying on the veranda and if possible
to discover if any part of it could be eaten. Pigeons are like
children, always hungry, and very nosy. I sat up and looked
at the sky; it was cloudless, it would be a hot day. We had
brought our own rice and I went to the kitchen to cook it.
A fire was burning there already and a monk was busy
cutting up vegetables. A friendly man, whom I had met
before, he greeted me and gave me a small dish of radish
relish and a few preserved plums for my master's breakfast.
While I waited for my rice to cook, I watched him; he
handled the knife very deftly. The monks in the temple
were strict vegetarians, and poor Goro would get neither
fish nor squid there.

"Your master is satisfied with his rooms?" the monk
asked. I nodded, while I wondered if I could ever be
a monk. I thought not, but then I didn't know what I
could or wanted to become; maybe I would be, like
Matsu, a servant forever. "Did you get up very early?" I
asked.

"At sunrise. We follow the sun; we go to bed when it

sets and get up when the sun gets out of bed." The monk nodded. "To serve Buddha."

To serve Buddha, I repeated to myself. What exactly did those words mean? They came so glibly over many men's tongues, as if everyone knew what they meant, but surely it did not mean the same to everyone. My rice was nearly cooked, so I went to see if my master was awake.

By midafternoon all the Ako retainers that my master had expected had arrived. They had prayed at the tomb of their Lord, as fervently as if he really were buried there. Now they all were seated in the big room, eighteen of them, two of whom had come all the way from Ako; the rest were either living in Osaka or in Kyoto. I had been serving them tea, in cups we had borrowed from the temple. I wondered if I was going to be allowed to stay, though it did not matter much for I would find out later what had taken place. I knew that a message, a letter, had come from Edo, but not what it contained or whom it was from.

Oishi-sama had taken out the letter when he noticed me kneeling by the door; I could read on his face that he was making up his mind whether he should let me stay or not. He raised his fan and pointed toward the door behind me; I bowed and left.

Once outside I thought of listening at the door, but decided against it. Instead, I left the house altogether and went into the garden. An old monk was busy cleaning up the garden, which was spotless. He picked up leaves that had fallen from the bushes and trees; since it was not yet autumn there were not many. By the pond I sat down on a favorite large stone and watched the fish. A carp of great size and age swam slowly by, hardly moving its tail. Surely the carp is the laziest of fish. It stuck its head nearly out of the water, its mouth opening and closing as if it were saying its prayers.

"We feed them," a voice said near me. It was the old monk. "He was there when I came." The monk pointed to the old fish who was heading for the center of the pond. "He was smaller then, but still not tiny. It is said that they can live to a great age."

"They are very beautiful," I said. A silver one was now coming toward me. "They move so slowly."

"They teach us that very few things in life are worth hurrying for." The old monk chuckled. "That is why no path in the garden is ever straight. If you wander in a leisurely way the garden is very big, if you hurry it is small. We want you to walk slowly and that is why the path turns and twists itself like a snake." The old monk walked off to pick up more leaves. I watched him for a while; he too moved sedately, like a carp. At my feet lay a tiny pebble. I thought of picking it up to throw into the pond, but decided not to, as I was afraid it might offend the old man or possibly even the big carp.

I entered the temple. I could smell the incense, which was always burning near the altar. I knelt down and looked at the statue of Buddha; he stared back at me, a tiny smile curling his lips. From the temple a roofed corridor connected the building where our rooms were. I walked as slowly as the carp had swum; noiselessly I slid back the door. Now I could see to the very end of the corridor that ran in back of the rooms. Outside the door to our place a figure was kneeling. It was one of the youngest monks in the temple. I watched him for a while. Then I closed the door behind me as if I had just come in. The monk rose and almost ran toward me. As he came near me he began explaining what could not be explained. "I thought your master, having many guests, might be in need of something."

I shook my head but said nothing; then as I passed him as I walked on, I could hear him opening and then closing the door. *Another spy,* I thought as I sat down outside the door. It was better that I guarded it.

As soon as the meeting was over I told my master what I had seen. "He had been listening there maybe a long time," I said. "The excuse he gave was silly and he knew it."

"He does not only serve Buddha but others as well. But it is good to know that he might be in Kira's pay. If he is Kira's ear here, we can let him know what we want Kira to know. He learned little this time."

"There is a boy here who told me that the priest is very greedy for money." I thought of Goro and wondered if he had gotten beaten for eating the rice. "His parents have sent him here to become a monk, but he has little liking for that life."

"I am taking the others into the town, to eat" — Oishi-sama paused for a moment, then said — "and to drink some sake. I shall probably be late coming back. Talk to the boy or any of the monks who serve here as freely as you need to. Tell them that you think I have no plans but to retire from life, to say my prayers before I die."

I nodded and he joined the others. I watched them leave the temple grounds. *Some of them are hungry,* I thought, *and a few of them have had sake to drink.* The life of ronin is difficult, and I wondered if any of them had hidden their swords and taken work which they were ashamed of. I went to the room to clean it and take the cups that belonged to the temple back to the kitchen.

I ate the leftover rice from the morning for my supper, made rice balls out of it, which saved me from cooking. Then as I could not find Goro I drifted out into the part of the town near the temple. As this was the outskirts of the town there wasn't much to see. I passed some entrance gates that made me realize that many very rich people must be living in Kyoto. I wondered who they were, if they were related to the Emperor. A palanquin was carried by; beside the bearers four samurai were guarding it. I had fallen on my knees and bowed my head as it passed. When I rose and glanced after the litter, wondering who was inside it, I noticed a man who seemed to be watching me.

I walked faster and turned down the first side road I came to. When I had walked a little way I stopped and looked back. The man was following me. *It's only by chance he is going the same way,* I said to myself while I hurried on. At the next crossroad I turned in the direction I thought would lead me back to the temple. I hadn't gone far when I heard him shouting for me to stop. Without knowing why, I obeyed. The man was walking very fast toward me. *Should I run? And could I outrun him?* I was so frightened that I stayed, which was foolish. I should have tried to escape. The man was a samurai and they don't like to run, not in public.

"Down." The samurai pointed with his sword to the ground in front of him. In the twilight the blade glittered evilly. I knelt and looked up at him. He was a youngish man, his clothes not those of a rich person. He was not, I felt certain, an important retainer in the household of the lord he served.

"You are a servant of Oishi Kuranosuke?" he asked and I nodded in reply. "What is the purpose of your master renting rooms in the temple?"

"I don't know, sir." The tip of the samurai's sword was pointed at my throat. "He came to pray for his master, the Lord of Ako."

"There is no lord by the name of Asano anymore. Oishi Kuranosuke is a ronin; he is masterless so he cannot pray for his master." The samurai sneered. "Tell him to pray to Buddha for his own soul."

"I shall." I bowed my head low until my forehead touched the ground.

"Look up at me," the samurai ordered. "You servant boys all look alike — I must mark you so I can remember you." The tip of his sword touched my forehead; it did not hurt. The samurai turned and walked away. I put my hand to my temple — it came away all bloody.

"You will have a scar," said the old monk who had bandaged my head. "But many girls think that a man is handsomer because of such. It was not deep and it was clean. How did it happen?"

I shrugged my shoulder. "A samurai wanted to test if his sword was sharp enough," I finally muttered, while I thought, *I shall remember his face even without a mark on it.*

"They are but fools. Keep away from them, especially when they have drunk sake."

I agreed and went to lie down, for now my wound had begun to hurt a little.

·13·

Otaka Gengo

"He asked you if you were my servant?" Oishi-sama demanded.

"Yes," I mumbled. My master had been told what had happened by one of the monks and had woken me. "He said he wanted to mark me so that he could recognize me again."

"He knew what he was after; if you wound the servant you wound his master. It was an insult meant for me. What did he look like?"

"He was young, and I think his purse was light. I should know him if I saw him again, but he is hard to describe because . . . because he was so ordinary. He was not tall, but not short either, he was neither fat nor thin, as for his features . . ." I frowned. "Still, I shall never forget him. He needs no mark on his forehead for me to recall him."

"If you see him tell me immediately . . . Yet I shall do nothing, let them think what they want, and maybe that is exactly what I want." Oishi-sama smiled for a moment, then, as if he suddenly realized that I had been hurt, he asked, "Is it painful?"

I shook my head, though in truth it was, but I did not

want him to know it. If you kick someone's dog the owner will object because the dog is his, not because he cares that the dog has been hurt. I had been hurt because I was Oishi-sama's dog and that was why he was angry. If I had belonged to someone else, he might have found the matter not even worthy of a frown. My master went into his room, where I had spread out his bedding, and I lay down again, hoping that I would be able to fall asleep.

When I woke in the morning my wound hurt much less. Some days later it itched as it healed, which can keep you awake. We walked back to Yamashina, arriving there about noon. When my mother saw my bandaged head she asked what had happened. I told her, describing it in such detail that I finally became aware that she had long ago stopped listening.

"It doesn't matter," she said as I finished my tale. I never found out what didn't matter, as I didn't ask her. If I had, I should probably not have been any the wiser. Matsu was much more concerned than my mother had been. After I had told my story, he said, "Jiro, I am sorry you got hurt. You are a good boy and, I am sure, loyal to our master. Think of your wound as an honor. A wound received for the sake of Oishi-sama."

I agreed that I would, though I was certain I wouldn't. But Matsu would have been shocked if I had told him what I really felt, that to my master I meant no more than a dog, a horse, or a favorite pet bird.

As I had thought, it didn't take long for me to find out what had happened at the meeting in the temple. Chikara, on the very day after we had come home, told me. First I had to tell him how I got my wound. My story excited him so much that he demanded that if I saw the samurai again, I was not to tell his father but warn him instead and he would fight him. I promised this, though it was a promise I was not intending to keep.

"It was a letter from Edo, from someone very near the Shogun. He said he would try to speak to him and plead that Lord Asano's brother should be allowed to be head of the Ako clan. My father is worried that some of our men who are in Edo will attack Kira and spoil any chance the Asano family has of retaining Ako castle."

"Will your father travel to Edo?" I asked. The thought of going there excited me. I had heard many stories about the town, and felt certain that if my master went, he would take me.

"No, he sent Ushioda Matanojo and Nakamura Kansuke up to calm them and also Hara Soemon, though it is a long journey for someone as old as he is. But maybe my father will go later; I hope if he does he will take me." Chikara looked far from certain that this would happen. He was a good youngster, though at present he was more playing at being a samurai than actually being one. We had been friends when we were small; then he liked to act as if he was one of the famous samurai that his father had told him about, and he would strut around the garden brandishing his bamboo sword. I was then his retainer, though sometimes I was allowed a different role in our games, a villain but never a hero.

After a week my wound had healed enough for me to

discard the bandage. A long red line disfigured my fore-head, but as I was not handsome in the first place, I consoled myself with the thought that it made me look more inter-esting. My mother said that my head looked like a cracked egg.

By the beginning of the ninth month the worst of the summer heat was over. I was sitting outside the gate of our house when a samurai coming from the east stopped and peered at me. "I have seen you somewhere before, boy," he said and shook his head wonderingly. "At Ako castle," I said, for I had recognized him. His name was Otaka Gengo and he was one of Lord Asano's retainers that I had always liked.

"You are right, the very place." Otaka-sama smiled. He was not a very handsome man, neither old nor young, but Matsu told me that a girl had drowned herself for love of him. He was rather splendidly dressed, though his clothes were none too clean, and his straw sandals were worn and his feet very dirty, as if he had walked far. But what was most unusual was his companion, a white dog that he led on a leash. When he noticed that I was staring at it, he said, "This is my new master; I grew tired of being a ronin; he is called Inu-sama and" — he lowered his voice to a whisper — "he is a friend of the Shogun."

I looked at Lord Dog, who had seated himself and was moving his fleas around with the help of his rear leg. Our Shogun is a very strict Buddhist and has made laws against killing or mistreating animals, and at great expense he has made homes for old dogs and horses, where they are kept until they die. Some people are very angry about this, and claim that he is mad. But making fun of the Shogun is not very safe, for he is not known to have much sense of humor.

"What happened to your head? Did you fall down from the roof?" The samurai looked at the gate and house beyond it. "A very handsome place."

"Someone cut me," I said and told him the story.

"Lucky for him that it was only a child he cut. Now if it had been Inu-sama here he had wounded, he would have ended his life on the execution grounds." Otaka-sama shook his head in mock sorrow. "Would you be so kind as to take me and Inu-sama to your master? I shall let you lead him." With those words he handed me the leash that was attached to the dog's collar. "Remember, if he bites you, you are not allowed to bite him back."

It was still hot and my master was sitting under a tree in the garden; he had placed a bench there in its shade. When he saw who had arrived, he immediately rose and bowed. I watched them greet each other, Oishi-sama bending just that fraction less than the younger samurai. After having asked each other the state of their health and exchanged greetings, my master finally noticed the dog. The animal was sitting down beside me and looking at him. "What is that?" he asked and pointed at it. The dog rose and wagged its tail.

Otaka-sama began a long tale about how he had acquired the dog, saying that now he had taken service with it, as its chief retainer. I could see that the joke was not to my master's liking. Finally he interrupted him, saying, "Do you never get tired of playing the fool, Otaka Gengo?"

"Why should I," Otaka-sama replied, "when the highest in the country do not mind doing it? Who made us ronin, but a fool?"

My master held up his hand to stop the younger man. "A samurai is concerned about his own behavior, not that of his master or those above him. Like you, I think certain decrees unwise, but if every man believes he knows best how to rule the country, it will not be ruled. I ask you as a retainer of Lord Asano to stop this nonsense."

"If you wish me to, I shall. Still it seems hard for me to understand that a samurai who by mistake has killed a bird, a swallow I believe, was condemned to commit seppuku, whereas someone can disfigure this boy without being punished."

"The Shogun has a nickname, you know what it is?" Oishi-sama lowered his voice. "He is called Inu-kubo, the Shogun of the dogs. Still we must obey him, not because we honor him, but because we respect and honor his title. Jiro, tie that dog up somewhere, but not where he can dig up the flowers, and give him some water and scraps from the kitchen."

I was about to obey when my master beckoned me to wait. "Have some sake brought and something to munch while we drink it. I think Otaka-sama prefers it to tea."

I bowed and smiled as I left. Otaka-sama was known to like sake, and he too, like the Shogun, had a nickname; it was Tanuki. That is a sly little animal that lives in the woods and has a reputation for liking rice wine. Most men, though they will not admit it, are secretly proud to be compared to it.

I told one of the young maids in the kitchen to bring sake into the garden. I made sure that she served something good to eat — plums, two kinds of pickles, and mushrooms as well. I wanted the very best for Otaka-sama, for he at least put me above a dog.

·14·

On the Road to Edo

"We are taking you along to Edo; Oishi-sama says you are useful. Are you?" Otaka-sama looked at me.

"I try to be." I didn't know that my master had decided to travel to Edo. It was the middle of the tenth month and the leaves were turning. We were sitting in the garden under some trees; the dog was lying at our feet.

"To be useful, full of use, I suppose no one can deny that that is a good thing. Take Inu-sama here, he is rather the opposite, of no use whatsoever." The dog, hearing its name, glanced up at its master. Otaka-sama did not add the word *sama*, lord, to the dog's name when my master could hear it.

"But many people keep dogs," I argued, "so they must be of some use."

"What is useful or not useful depends upon whether you think it so. If you like to wear clothes of silk, then you will deem silk useful. If your concern is merely to keep warm, you might not. As for dogs, if you like the sight of a wagging tail and to have your hand licked, then I suppose they are useful." With those words he held out his hand, and Inu-sama dutifully rose to lick it.

"And you like it?" I said, laughing. "So the dog is useful." Otaka-sama was living in the temple above our house and a great deal of the time he was so bored that he would seek me out to talk to. It was very strange for me, for he treated me not so much as an equal, but as if I were some kind of favorite retainer that he had acquired.

"One must not despise love, even from a dog. Love is precious, Jiro." Otaka-sama laughed, and his laughter made me dare to ask him if we were going to Edo to kill Kira-sama.

Surprised, Otaka Gengo looked at me and then laughed. "I wish we were. But don't add 'sama,' Kira will do for him."

"Why are we going then?" I asked.

For a moment Otaka-sama looked pensively at me, as if he was deciding if he could trust me. "At present Kira's house is so well protected that it would be madness to attack it. Yet some of the younger samurai are so hot-tempered that they might attempt it on their own. It is to prevent such foolishness and to knock some sense into a couple of heads that we have to travel to Edo."

I nodded, then asked, "When you do kill Kira, what will happen to you and to my master?"

"We shall kill Kira in order to set something right; one cannot tolerate injustice. As for what will happen to us, that will be up to the Shogun, though I believe we shall need more than one Kaishaku-nin. They are hard to find these days, most samurai having grown too soft and their swords too dull to perform that office."

I knew that the Kaishaku-nin, usually a friend of the

man who was committing seppuko, cut off the head of the person after he had slit his belly. The thought made me shiver and Otaka-sama noticed it.

"A samurai lives with death; it is his companion from the time he first sticks his swords into his obi. A love of death and a love of life are the two balls we juggle: one is golden, like the sun, the other silver, like the moon. Life is only a preparation for death, Jiro. The law of the samurai is not to fear the silver ball in spite of loving the golden one."

At that moment someone called "Jiro!" I looked toward the house; it was my mother. "Go and be useful," Otaka-sama said and grinned.

Water was needed and I had to carry some bucketfuls from the well. In a way, I was the lowest servant of all in the house; even the youngest of the girls who served my master's wife were older and ordered me about. True, I had no particular duties, but that only meant that I could be set to do anything. Oishi-sama used me as a messenger, which meant he trusted me above some of the other servants, but that did not really give me a special position. Rank means as much in the servant quarters as it does anywhere else. I was the youngest member and my mother, in spite of her age, was looked down upon by all. Still I was far from misused. I had made a habit of doing anything I was asked to do willingly. I thought that since I would have to do it in any case I might as well do it cheerfully and because of that receive some credit for it. My mother was always grumbling, and no one was ever grateful, even when she had done her work well.

We were to walk to Edo. Otaka-sama declared it could be done in a couple of weeks but we would wear out some straw sandals doing it. I knew that I would not be given a horse in any case, but it might mean I would have to carry something. Another servant was supposed to come as well to carry a load, but Oishi-sama decided against it. So each of the samurais carried a bundle containing clothes and food for the first few days. "We shall travel faster without servants; I have always found that they slow you down," my master declared. I am not sure that the others agreed, but they did not complain. I think they would have preferred that my master had hired horses.

The party consisted of three samurai in addition to my master and Otaka-sama. Of the three there was one I did not like, whose name was Okuno Shokan. He was the kind of man who would not dream of thanking an inferior. I was so much beneath him that I was almost nonexistent. I say almost, for he certainly ordered me about enough, never calling me by my name. Once he hit me because my shadow fell on him.

The first few days on the road I was so tired by night that I walked the last few miles in my sleep. Since the road was the main one between Kyoto and Edo, there were plenty of inns along our route, so we slept under a roof and ate very well on our journey. We had to pass several checkpoints, where officers of the Shogun would question the travelers and examine goods they were carrying. In this way the Tokugawa Shogunate kept an eye on the movements of everyone in Japan. You, or rather your master, had to carry papers with permission to travel and to bring along servants. We were allowed to go right through most of them; only at the checkpoint at Hakone were we troubled and there even our baggage was searched.

I had been instructed by my master to answer anyone who asked me who my master was and where we were heading that he was a samurai on an errand for his lord. But no one asked me; even most servants found it beneath their dignity to talk to a mere boy like me. I was not poorly dressed; I had been given clothing by my master (I think they were clothes that Chikara had outgrown).

The nearer we came to Edo, the longer our daily march became, which meant that though I got more accustomed to walking, I was equally tired when the sun grew low in the horizon. Being the only servant, I walked by myself, though at times Otaka-sama would slow down his steps and talk to me. He was ever cheerful and seemed to thrive on the day's journey. Okuno-sama had reprimanded him for talking to me, and for generally talking too much. "A samurai is as sparing in the use of words as he is in all other things," he had said and then added, "and, as for one's inferiors, one does not notice them unless one has use for them."

"I thought of telling him that you are useful, and that I use you to sharpen my wits on, just as one uses a whetstone to sharpen one's sword. But on second thought there is no point to it; he is too old to learn and I, in his eyes, too young to teach him." Then Otaka-sama laughed and, pointing to a bird in the sky, told me what it was called.

Two days before our arrival in Edo we were staying in an inn so crowded with travelers seeking shelter for the night that it was overflowing. Our party was told to bed down in the entrance hall as all rooms were taken. The hall had a wooden floor and some old mats were laid down for everyone to sleep on. Unfortunately, Okuno Shokan found out that one of the rooms had been given to a wealthy merchant, and when he saw food being carried there and heard laughter, he became furious. Oishi-sama tried to calm him down, for he did not want trouble. He wanted to enter Edo as unobtrusively as possible. But Okuno-sama drew the shorter of his swords and, grabbing the owner of the inn by his clothes, tickled his throat with it, while he explained the order of rank. "If there is no room in the inn, then merchants should sleep outside."

"My lord!" the innkeeper said and fell on his knees. "A mistake has been made, I shall see to it that you get the room."

I don't know where the merchant slept, but if anyone slept in a ditch I am sure it was the innkeeper himself. Our party was given the room which the merchant and his two servants had occupied. The merchant was so frightened that he ordered and paid for sake to be brought to my master and his friends.

The incident almost cost me a beating. I had been told to get what rest I could in a shed. Now I had to share it with, among others, the merchant's servants. They were obviously important men, as their clothes showed, and not used to being sent to such poor quarters. Other servants were there as well, including one who had led the merchant's packhorse. I think he was not fond of washing, for he smelled much of the animal he was in charge of. I stayed silently in a corner, wondering if it was not best that I leave. The youngest of the merchant's servants carried a small dagger in his obi, and he drew it out and contemplated it. I acted as if I did not notice it; only samurai were allowed to carry weapons. I'm sure he knew that, but if he didn't I wasn't going to tell him. The older servant motioned for him to put it away, and he stuck it once more into his obi. It was so small the sash hid it.

"Who is your master?" the older servant asked me. I answered as I had been told to, a samurai from the west country traveling to Edo on business for his lord.

"His master must be so poor that he cannot afford to give him a horse," the younger one said sneeringly.

"Our lord has many horses, it was our choice to travel by foot," I said, hoping that they would leave me alone.

"I say your master serves no lord, he is merely a ronin, maybe discharged for being dishonest. He is better at bragging than at working. Is he a highwayman? Is that how he makes his living, your precious master?" The young servant rose, like a cat waiting to spring.

"We are only travelers like yourself and your master. We wish no harm to anyone," I said, putting on a carefree air I didn't feel.

"This must be a kennel, since they allow dogs in here. I will not share my lodging with a puppy like you, even if you wag your tail." Grabbing a stick that was standing by the door, which the leader of the packhorse had used to beat his animal with, he brandished it at me. I was just about ready to try to make my escape when I noticed that the door was being silently slid open. Otaka-sama stood just outside, one hand resting on the hilt of his sword, his face split in a wide grin.

"Jiro, I was afraid that you might catch fleas in such low

company, so I have come to get you. You can sleep in front of our door, and so guard us against these thieves from the marketplace."

I ran quickly to him. He had heard everything and even seen most of it through a crack in the wall. He looked for a moment down at the hilt of his sword, as if he contemplated drawing it. "What is it you have in your obi?" he asked of the young servant. "I should cut you down for breaking the law, but I don't care to dirty the blade of my sword with a pig's blood. Hand me that knife!"

Submissively the young man bowed his head and drew the dagger from where it was hidden in his obi, handing it by its point to Otaka-sama. He drew it from its sheath, looked at it with contempt, and then stuck it deep into the earthen floor of the shed and with his foot broke it.

When we were out of earshot Otaka-sama laughed. "Jiro, it would not have been a fair fight, for his steel, though poor, was better than mine." He drew his own sword from his obi. Only the hilt was real; the rest of it was a piece of clumsy wood of no use whatsoever. "I have a furious temper, Jiro, so don't cross me. I have often lost it but unfortunately I always find it again." Otaka-sama grinned at me. "So I thought it best not to carry my swords, as I might be tempted to use them. It wouldn't help our revenge over the injustice done to our lord for me to have been involved in a silly brawl."

As I lay down to sleep next to the door of my master's room, I couldn't help smiling at the thought of Otaka-sama's weapon. Though we started our journey as soon as the sun had risen, the merchant and his servant must have gotten up even earlier, for they were gone when we rose.

·15·

Two Officers
of the Shogun

"Having a temper is rather like having a dog loose inside you. It lies peacefully sleeping, but at the least commotion it starts to bark. A true samurai should be in complete control of himself at all times, Jiro." Otaka-sama shook his head. "He should bark, not the dog inside him." I looked up at the samurai; he had fallen back in order to speak to me. I felt like saying, a true samurai must never be intimate with his inferior. Maybe my face mirrored my thought, for Otaka-sama suddenly asked me what I was thinking about. I hesitated for a moment but then I told him and he laughed.

"You are right, Jiro. But at the present moment I am feeling pretty inferior myself, so maybe it can be overlooked."

"You never seem to get angry at me, and I'm sure I'm not a good servant," I said.

"I would never become angry at someone for making a mistake, or for being clumsy. Why, anyone can make a mistake and anyone can be clumsy. No, it is when I see some mean act, someone doing something out of spite, or merely showing his strength because someone else is weaker. That is when I get angry and lose my temper. My father, long dead, once said to me, 'Gengo, the ills of the world are no concern of yours.' I agreed, for it's true, one should be concerned only with what concerns one."

"But you are going to avenge an insult that is not yours, but your lord's." We were getting nearer Edo, and there were more and more travelers on the road.

"No, an insult to one's lord is an insult to his retainers. If there is not loyalty to your lord and to your clan, then the word *samurai* should cease to be. The lord and the clan are greater than you; you exist because of them, without them you are nothing. If we are not loyal, everything will fall apart and the strong and the cruel will rule. Highwaymen will inherit our swords." Two merchants riding splendid horses and followed by a whole line of packhorses passed us on their way to Kyoto or Osaka. Otaka-sama gave them a look of disgust, then suddenly hurried ahead to catch up with the others.

If everything fell apart would it matter to me? I wondered, and decided it would not. I always kept so far behind my master that I wouldn't be able to hear what he said to his companions, on the other hand close enough so that he could call me. Besides a few things of my own, I carried a bundle strapped to my back, containing my master's best kimono and some other clothes of his. The bundle was not heavy, but I was always glad to get rid of it when we reached an inn in the evening.

As we entered Edo we passed a field of execution. These were always close to a road so that the sight of the heads of the criminals fixed on stakes would help to deter others from crime. I wondered if it did. I didn't want to look at it, yet I knew I would. A raven was sitting on one of the heads. *Food for ravens and crows, could it happen to me? Yes, it could,* I mumbled, answering my own question. *Maybe when the world falls apart.*

The inn where we stayed was humble enough. It was near the river; as a matter of fact, it was built right on the riverbank. At times, especially in the summer, the river didn't have a pleasant smell as it was used as a sewer and place to deposit garbage.

Still, it fascinated me because of the boats. Some had come from Osaka and I even saw one that had come from Ako. The innkeeper was a decent man. He came from Harima and I think my master knew him. My master and his companions were given a room overlooking the river. It was the largest in the inn, with the advantage of being a corner room, which meant that there was less chance of being overheard. I would sleep outside the door and would eat in the kitchen. Two samurai had the room next to ours. I did not care for them and thought they might be spies of Kira's. Though the inn was not large, there were several rooms and all of them empty. I had heard the two samurai insisting that they wanted a river room, and the only river room left was the one next to ours. I told my master about my suspicion, and he nodded to indicate that he had heard me, but he said nothing.

Two of the samurai who had traveled with us to Edo left after our evening meal, to lodge in other places. One was Okuno Shokan. I was not sorry to see him go and neither I think was Otaka-sama. Being much older, Okuno-sama often complained that the young men of today did not show proper respect to their elders, and then glanced over at Otaka-sama to make sure that he had understood whom he meant. He was a tyrant to servants and a tiresome man to his equals. The one who stayed, besides Otaka-sama, was too fond of food and sake to be very concerned about his dignity. He was a good singer and when he had enough sake inside him, he would sing songs of the countryside where he had been born.

The next day, as soon as breakfast had been served to them, my master and his companions left for Sengakuji temple, where Lord Asano was buried. There they were to meet some of the younger Asano samurai. I was told to stay in the inn, a command that I obeyed for a while, but then the noises and shouts from the street grew too tempting for me. The streets of Edo are not laid out in the same straight and orderly manner as the streets of Kyoto. They wiggle along like snakes, crossing each other at strange angles. It is easy to get lost and therefore I kept close to the river. Everywhere people were selling things, not only in stores but in the street as well. I must have looked not altogether poor, for several of the hawkers would call out to me to come and inspect their wares.

Edo is also different in that you see many more samurai and not nearly so many priests and monks as you do in Kyoto. The samurai are treated with much greater respect than I was used to seeing, but then Edo is the Shogun's city and Kyoto the Emperor's. I saw two samurai questioning a man. He had thrown himself upon the ground and every time he answered a question he would beat his forehead against the ground. I didn't find out what he had done, for I dared not linger. Maybe because of this incident I decided to return to the inn.

As I took off my straw sandals in the entrance hall I noticed that one of the young servant girls looked at me in a strange way and then ran off. This made me hurry down to our room. Quickly I slid the door open. The two samurai from the next room were sitting on the tatami floor slowly looking through my master's possessions. I was just about to close the door again when the older of them said, "Come in, boy."

It was a command and I obeyed, though I stayed as near the door as I dared. I knelt and bowed and waited.

"You are Oishi Kuranosuke's servant." It was not a question but a statement. I bowed my head agreeing but said nothing.

"Your master has turned down several offers that most masterless samurai would have been only too eager to agree to."

"I don't know that," I mumbled. "I am only the least of the servants in his house."

"You have ears and eyes, I believe." The younger of the two laughed spitefully. "We are officers of the Shogunate. I presume you know what that is?"

"Yes, your honor," I said and bowed, letting my forehead touch the tatami mat three times.

"Where is your master? Answer, boy!" the older samurai demanded.

"My master Oishi-sama went to pay his respects and to pray at his master's tomb. He was the chief retainer of the lord of Ako." To my surprise I realized that I was getting angry. *If I had been a samurai,* I thought, *I would need a wooden sword as well.*

"I know your master's position. You need not tell me what it was. What you have seen you may tell him. As a matter of fact it is your duty to tell him. Unfaithful servants are a curse, worse than fleas. You may tell him, too, that no one wishes him any harm, yet it is wise for him to keep in mind that the punishment for forming secret groups conspiring together to disturb the public peace is death."

"I shall, your honor," I said and bowed again, letting my forehead touch the mat.

The two samurai rose, and I moved sideways on all fours, like a crab, to get out of their way. As he stood in the door the older man said, "To you, boy, your master is a great and important man, and his former master Asano almost a god. But remember that to the Shogun, Lord Asano was a mere shadow and your master no more than the leaves that fall from the trees now in the autumn."

I stayed kneeling until I was sure they had gone. I couldn't help wondering — *If Oishi-sama is no more than a dead leaf, what am I?*

·16·

The Silk-Clad Actor

"There is no doubt about it, Jiro, you should have been born a dog." Otaka-sama looked at me as if I could possibly be turned into such an animal without too much trouble. We were sitting in the tiny garden of the inn.

"Why? I don't really think I would like being a dog." I smiled at the young samurai.

"Then you could have bitten those two spies of Kira and they wouldn't have dared to do anything to you." Otaka-sama nodded several times in agreement with himself. "In our times it is better to be a dog than a man. If Lord Asano had bitten Kira instead of drawing his sword, the Shogun would not have demanded that he commit seppuku."

I couldn't help laughing at the thought of Lord Asano biting Kira, and at the same time I was surprised that Otaka-sama dared say something like that. Suddenly it occurred to me that maybe that was the sort of thing that men said to their wives or their pet dogs, things they didn't dare say to anyone else. Otaka-sama was unmarried and the dog Inu-sama was left at home in Yamashina. But whether I was a substitute for a wife or the dog, I wasn't sure.

"They said they had come from the Shogun, not from

Kira," I reminded him. "And I am sure of one thing: any dog that bit either of them would not have lived to bark about it."

"You're probably right. I wish it was over and done with. Waiting is hard for a man of my temperament."

"What if Lord Asano's brother is made a lord . . . What if he is given the title, maybe even made Daimyo of Ako?" I asked, for I know my master had petitioned the Shogun for this.

Otaka-sama made a wry face. "I don't think that will happen, but if it did we would no longer be ronin. We would have a master and our duty would be to obey him."

"Then Kira would not be punished and his insult not avenged?" I asked.

"Probably not, but the Shogun will not change his mind, unless his mother should change it for him. And that will not happen, because, being low-born, she hates all the samurai in Japan. She likes only sutra-chanting priests. Still the revenge will have to wait until word has come that our petition has been refused. Your master is a patient man; such men are good at fishing, too." Otaka-sama smiled. "I was not given that gift when I was born; still, though it comes hard to me, I must learn it . . . When I was young and first learned to write I found that hard, too, but I mastered it. Can you read or write, Jiro?"

"No," I said, though I could recognize a few signs, but I wouldn't know how to draw them.

"You must learn it, Jiro. Then get work with some merchant. Don't serve a samurai again. Learn to count money, to buy and sell, for that is where the future lies. The signs were not invented in China for the sake of writing poetry. Have you ever written a poem, Jiro?"

"I told you, I can't write," I reminded him.

"Dogs bark at the moon, and cats, too, when the stars come out, are not silent. Have you not thought a poem? One need not write them down."

"No, not really. At least I don't think so." Confused, I looked down upon the ground. I felt Otaka-sama's hand on my shoulder.

"I think that someday you will, Jiro," he said, and walked into the inn.

The meeting with the Asano ronin who lived in Edo was not held at the inn, but at some other place in the town. Where, I never discovered; suddenly my master had become very silent whenever I was near. I felt a little hurt, for after all, the scar I had on my forehead was the mark of a wound I had received in his service. Maybe he felt it, for as he and Otaka-sama went out one evening he said to me, "What you do not know, child, you cannot tell others."

I bowed in reply, meaning with that motion of my body that I understood. But did I really? I went to the kitchen and a maid made me some tea. She was young and not very pretty.

"Your young master is very funny," she said and laughed.

"That he is," I agreed.

"Is he married?" she asked and held her hand in front of her mouth as she said it.

"I don't think so." With surprise, I watched her cheeks redden as she blushed. *That girl is full of dreams,* I thought, and smiled at her. "The two samurai that took the room next to my master's, did you know them?"

"How could I know them?" The girl shook her head and I realized that she had misunderstood me.

"I mean, have you ever seen them before?" I asked. "They were a little too important to lodge in an inn like this."

"Oh no, I have never seen them before, never ever." The poor girl looked so miserable that I felt certain that the samurai had not only questioned her, but possibly even paid her a few copper coins to keep her eyes open.

"It doesn't matter, I just wondered if you had." I looked reassuringly at her and said with a smile, "I am sure Otaka-sama is not married."

"It doesn't really matter. I wouldn't care if he was. It is just that I wanted to know." Again she blushed and then ran from the room, as if she had suddenly thought of something she had to do.

I thought, *Otaka-sama throws thank yous around wherever he goes, which makes him popular. She has many dreams and if he is not married then she can marry him in her dreams. But if he was, she would have to find someone else to dream about.* Suddenly the thought came to me that my mother must have looked a little like that girl when she was very young, not pretty but yet still containing some girlishness that had made her attractive. Attractive to whom? Who was my father? — an old thought, an old question, to which I probably should never get an answer. But a girl like this one in the inn, or my mother, any samurai could pick up at will, and drop when finished with her. I felt my cheeks flush. *Better not think about it,* I admonished myself as I walked out into the street. The sun was setting, the sky on fire in the west. There were still many people about and I drifted with the crowd. Soon I was in a quarter where I hadn't been before, and a great many people were emerging from a building larger than the others in the street. On the façade of the house were signs, but I couldn't read them. They looked like lists of words. Suddenly a man came from the building, so splendidly dressed that I was surprised, for he wore no swords. His kimono was silk, that was certain, and he was followed by a servant almost as splendidly dressed. Everyone made way for him and many of the people bowed.

"Who is he?" I asked a man standing near me.

"He is an actor. Ichikawa Danjuro, some say he is the greatest of them all." The man smiled at me.

"An actor . . ." I didn't really know what the word meant.

"Yes, and he can act anything, there is no part he cannot play." The man was still looking in the direction where the actor had disappeared and the expression on his face was one of wonder and pleasure. "See!" He pointed to the billboards on the building. "His name is the first on the list." Then suddenly aware that he was talking to a mere boy, he asked, "And where do you come from?"

"From the west, your honor," I answered, "from Ako."

"You have no theater there, I'm sure."

"But we live in Yamashina now," I argued, "and that is close to Kyoto where the Emperor lives."

"But here in Edo the Shogun resides, and he is the master

of us all." The man walked away; he had wasted enough time with a mere boy from the country.

As I walked back toward the inn I thought, *I must ask Otaka-sama about the theater.* For some reason the sight of the silk-clad actor had excited me, as if it had some kind of meaning beyond what my eyes had seen.

·17·

We Return to Yamashina

"Yes, Jiro, I've been to the theater. There is one in Kyoto as well and I believe two in Osaka. The first time I went, I almost drew my sword and jumped up onto the stage. There was a villain on the stage that I would have loved to cut down. A wicked schemer, a terrible rogue, he made me so angry that I boiled with rage. But he was only an actor playing his part. A young girl sitting near me noticed my anger and laughed at me." Otaka-sama smiled as he recalled it. "She was so pretty when she laughed, with dimples in her cheeks, that I forgave her right away. Next time I went, the same actor was playing the part of Yoshitsune, the greatest of all the warriors that ever lived . . . I wonder about such men, such actors, do they have souls as we do, or are their souls mirrors that reflect the part they act? The women, too, are acted by men, but how can they be women on the stage and men when they leave it? It's a strange world, Jiro." Otaka-sama shook his head.

"I should like to see it," I said. "The actor I saw was clad in silk. He had a servant with him and lots of people bowed as he went by."

"Jiro, there is a man who writes the plays for them. He

was born in the country, but he lives in Kyoto now. He is the puppetmaster. He takes any story that he hears about and writes it down. When we kill Kira, he will write down what we have done or someone else surely will. Then you will be able to go and see some actor reflecting my soul. I have thought about it, and it will happen." Otaka-sama looked proudly at me.

"He will be you or Oishi-sama and then you will be killing Kira again."

"Yes! When we are long dead we shall be killing Kira again and again. We shall live and yet not live." Otaka-sama frowned. "At best we shall have to slit our bellies . . . at worst if Inu-kubo or his mother gets mad enough over our deed we shall have our heads placed on stakes. I sometimes dream of that, the shame of it would kill my mother. A samurai must ever be prepared for death, but not that, not that." Otaka-sama stared out in front of himself as if he were contemplating his own head decorating a stake.

"I am afraid of dying," I said as I thought, *I'm a coward, and I'm not only afraid of death, I'm afraid of pain, too.*

"You're not a samurai, Jiro, so it doesn't matter. You weren't brought up not to fear death. My father, once when I was still a small child, showed me the blade of his sword and asked me to touch it. I did and cut my finger; the scar is still there." Otaka-sama looked at his finger. "Then he took my hand and let a drop of my blood fall on the shiny metal as he said, 'Someday this sword will be yours, for you are my eldest son. Don't ever shame it.' I bowed my head and kept my tears back, for to tell the truth I was very frightened. My father was a terribly proud man. He always had a servant with him who carried his purse, for he wouldn't touch money. He said that coins not only dirtied a man's hands, but his soul as well." Otaka-sama smiled. "That is probably why he died poor."

"He wanted you to cut your finger?" I asked, wondering what Otaka-sama had looked like as a child.

"Oh yes, he held the sword so I almost had to. I felt like crying when I saw the blood but I knew I wasn't allowed to, that he wouldn't want me to. So I didn't cry; a son of a samurai must early learn to hide his tears . . . Now I shall have no children of my own." Otaka Gengo looked sad, but then he smiled as he said, "But with my temper it's just as well."

"I think I should like to be an actor. Do you think I could become one?" As I asked I knew it was a silly question.

Otaka-sama looked at me. "With that scar on your forehead you could play a villain. If the scar had been on your shoulder you could play Kira once you have grown." Seeing the unhappy look on my face he immediately changed his expression. "Jiro, I know little about it, but actors are considered a low lot, even when they wear silk. No, become a merchant, that is where the future lies. Someday, money, not the two swords, will be the master of our country. But remember what my father said! Let the money dirty your hands, but never your soul."

I bowed my head in agreement. Since all the money I had in the world was three copper coins in my sleeve, I didn't think my soul was in any great danger at present. *I'm glad in a way that I'm not a samurai,* I thought to myself, but did not express that thought aloud.

"I think you will be going back tomorrow. Your master has succeeded in calming the hotheads." Otaka-sama picked up a pebble from the ground, threw it into the air, and caught it as it fell. "I shall not come but will be staying here. But we'll meet again very soon."

"Will you be coming to Yamashina again?" I asked and the eagerness in my voice made the samurai smile. He was the first grownup that I had really cared for.

"Since Kira sends spies all the way to Kyoto, I shall stay and spy on him." Otaka-sama smiled. "I've heard of a merchant who sells rare teacups and is a master of the tea ceremony. I shall be taught by him how to turn my cup, so that I can turn it, when the time comes, on Kira." I looked confused for I did not understand what he meant. Otaka-sama noticed it and patted my head, and then as he left to enter the inn he whispered, "That tea ceremony master is a friend of Kira's."

The next day, almost as soon as the sun had risen, we rose too, and after breakfast we left. Otaka-sama accompanied my master to the edge of the town. There, in a tiny tea-house, they drank a last cup together. I knew that Otaka-sama sympathized with that group of the Ako ronin who didn't want to wait too long to attack Kira, but at the same time respected my master's judgment. Oishi-sama's final words to him as they parted were, "Most battles have been won by men who were careful and had patience. Tokugawa Ieyasu did not win the country by losing his temper but by keeping it at all times."

"You are our leader." Otaka-sama bowed humbly as he

said this, and my master bowed as well and almost as deeply. When we had gone on a little while I turned around. Otaka-sama was still standing in the road watching us. I held up my hand and waved. Then I admonished myself, for it was unseemly for someone like me to wave at a samurai. When Otaka-sama saw my hand descend, he held up his and waved to me. My master saw it and frowned but said nothing.

For the first week of our journey homeward my master hardly spoke to me. He seemed at all times to be deep in thought, as if something worried him. He was not unfriendly, even asking me once, when we had walked very far, if I was tired. I answered yes, which made him smile and say, "Jiro, you are more truthful than wise. Even if you are near dropping dead of fatigue, you should say 'Not at all.' "

"So I should lie?" I asked.

"Most servants would."

"But how then can their master trust them?" I asked.

"Most masters don't." Oishi-sama laughed. "Can I trust you?"

"Yes." I nodded as I thought about it. "You can trust me to do my best, but not always that my best is good enough."

"I do trust you, Jiro, or I would not have taken you along. You liked Otaka Gengo?"

"Oh yes," I said so fervently that I made my master smile. "Everyone likes him."

"Not everyone." My master wrinkled his brow. "His temper sometimes brings him into trouble. But servants like him and dogs do, too."

My master had quickened his steps and walked ahead, indicating that he had no wish to say more to me. I followed thinking, *Children like Otaka-sama too, and those men who like children are usually kind to their servants as well.*

The last night before we reached Yamashina and our home, my master spoke to me again. I had brought him tea and was just about to retire when, with a wave of his hand, he indicated for me to stay. "Jiro, flower growing may not have been enough. I have not convinced Kira's spies that I have retired from the world . . . Possibly the best way is to enter into it." My master seemed to be speaking more to himself than to me. "It is good that I have a stomach for sake." He smiled and shook his head. "Jiro, if someone asks about me, from now on look sad and say that your master has taken to drinking. A man who grows peonies and putters around the garden and reads the sutras is still respectable. Still a possible danger. But a drunken fool, who throws his money about and disgraces his own name, is no danger to anyone." Seeing the puzzlement mirrored in my face, he said, "We shall visit the floating world, you and I." Then, frowning, he indicated that I could leave.

The floating world, I mumbled to myself as I lay down to sleep. That was the part of the town where men went to amuse themselves. In the houses there sake flowed, and women played the samisen. There, too, the theaters were. As I fell asleep I thought again of the silk-clad actor.

·18·

A Meeting in Kyoto

Kyoto can be very cold in winter. Shortly after we returned the wind turned into the northwest and brought a heavy snowfall with it. Ako, being farther south and on the eastern coast, is much warmer and I had seen snow only once in my life before. Then it had but stayed in the morning and melted before noon, but the snow that year in Kyoto stayed for several weeks; we hardly saw the sun, and on most days low black clouds covered the sky. I had no clothes fit for such weather and I froze most miserably. My mother grumbled incessantly, as if the cold weather had been sent solely to make her life miserable. There was no talk from my master's side about visiting the floating world. Everyone kept inside and as near a charcoal fire as possible.

By the middle of the second month the weather changed, and a meeting of the samurai of Kyoto and Osaka was scheduled for the fourteenth in the little temple in Kyoto. On the thirteenth my master and I set out for the temple. The sky was light blue and on our way I saw several plum trees in full flower. Servants, and the poor, who seldom find themselves near a burning brazier, are happy when spring arrives, for their clothes, or lack of them, are usually better suited for summer breezes than winter winds.

We had not been to the temple since our return and I was eager to find out if the acolyte Goro was still there, or if he had run away to Osaka. I did not see him around, and when I was preparing my master's supper I asked the old monk who had been kind to me before what had happened to him. He laughed. "Goro," he said, tasting the name, "has gone to join his four brothers. No doubt his head will soon, if not already, be decorating a stake as a warning to other thieves. He left here a month ago, taking with him a bagful of coins that belonged to Buddha, or our head priest, but at least not to him. He will visit the teahouses in Shimabara or possibly Osaka, until the last coin is spent, and then he will rob someone else. He might be lucky, but eventually he will be caught and marched to the execution field. There he will shed many tears, until the executioner will make that well dry with one swing of his sword."

I thought he was right; Goro would not succeed. He was a fool and to survive as a fool, you need rich doting parents. The purse he had stolen would soon be empty, and as the monk said, Goro would attempt to repeat his crime, trusting to luck. Somehow it made me feel a little sad; not that I had liked the boy much, but maybe because I, too, was a poor boy with little hope for my future.

My master retired early but I could not sleep. I wandered around the garden. The moon had come out and the tall pine trees cast long shadows. I knew the meeting tomorrow was important; again there was trouble with the younger samurai, keeping up their spirit of vengeance and at the same time convincing them of the necessity for caution and not acting heedlessly. I had heard my master discuss it with an older samurai. He had said that he had hoped that Otaka Gengo would have been able to calm them, which had made the older samurai say that Otaka Gengo found it so difficult to calm himself, he doubted if he was the right man to tame the temper of others.

Because I missed Otaka-sama I thought of him. Was it really worth giving up one's life merely to avenge one's master? I was near the grave that Oishi-sama had constructed to honor Lord Asano. Suddenly I heard a voice whispering "Jiro." I glanced around me, but could discover no one. Again the ghostly voice called "Jiro." Though I was frightened my voice did not shake as I said, "Who is there?" Once more the voice called "Jiro," but this time it broke into laughter and Otaka Gengo stepped out from among the trees.

"What is Oishi's little servant doing here — is he paying homage to our Lord?" he asked.

"No, I couldn't sleep." I looked toward the stone placed over the grave which contained only Lord Asano's state kimono. "It would not be seemly for me to do that," I answered.

"Sparrows and eagles do not mix." Otaka-sama nodded at the rightness of what he had said. "Is your master well?"

"He is very well, in spite of the cold weather that has forced him to stay in the house."

"In Edo the pails of water left overnight had ice on them in the morning. One needed not only charcoal fires but warm sake as well to keep alive."

I nodded in agreement, though I had had neither. The

full moon appeared to be resting on Otaka-sama's left shoulder. "Go and sleep, child," he said, "and dream you are wearing silk clothes."

I rose and bowed to him, then walked away toward the little pavilion that was ours. I slept in the corridor outside my master's room. As I slid the door open I looked back; Otaka-sama was standing in front of the grave, praying.

I woke early in the morning because I was cold. The sun had not risen yet, but the sky was clear and in the east a golden glow foretold a pleasant day. I went to the kitchen and got hot water for tea. The old monk was there, and he gave me breakfast for my master, miso soup and some greens and rice. My master was already up and fully dressed. I gathered up his bedding and put it away in its closet, then I put the food on a little table in front of him. "Jiro" — my master had been watching me working — "when the others come give tea to those who want it. When I nod my head it will be a signal for you to leave, but do not go far away. Stay near so that no ears that should not be listening will be able to."

I nodded and bowed to show that I had understood, then asked if he wished for more rice.

"No, it will do. At my age one does not have the appetite one had in one's youth. Have you eaten, Jiro?"

"Not yet, Master," I said.

"Go and eat. What you hear this afternoon must stay inside your head. I trust you, Jiro."

I was by the door; I knelt down and bowed so my forehead touched the matted floor. Then I said, "I shall be as mute as if I had no tongue." Then, because he trusted me,

I looked up and said, "But if I was ever tortured, Oishi-sama, I am not sure I should not speak."

My master smiled. "I must keep you near me then, Jiro, so that none of Kira's men can catch you. Now run and eat."

Again I bowed, and went to the kitchen for my own breakfast. I was glad that I had said what I had, for if he trusted me it was best that he knew that I was no hero who would die in pain with sealed lips.

In the early part of the afternoon all had come and the room was crowded with Lord Asano's retainers. I had been serving tea to those who wanted it, and everyone was talking, but mostly about unimportant things like the cold spell we had just experienced. Suddenly they all grew quiet. Oishi-sama looked toward me and nodded almost imperceptibly. I bowed in response and opening the door to the hallway I left, and closed it behind me.

Otaka-sama was the first to speak; eagerly he told what he had learned in Edo. It seemed that Lord Kira had retired from all official duties and it was rumored that he might be moving to Yonezawa, a district that was in the domain of his son, who had been adopted by the Uesugi family and now was Lord Uesugi. "Once he is there, he is safe and none of us can touch him." Otaka-sama's voice almost broke in eagerness. "No man can live under the same sky as the murderer of his father or his lord; therefore we must attack now while he still is within the reach of our swords." There was a mumble from those who agreed, but others spoke against it. My master remained silent. I guessed that among the men there were some he did not trust, whose only reason for staying was so they could claim a loyalty they had never really felt, if the Asano family was restored. I could imagine him, listening to every word said and watching the expressions on the faces of those who spoke. Every once in a while I would go outside and walk around the house to make certain that no one was there, spying on the meeting. Once I saw the old monk; he was not near the building, but some of the more rebellious of the Asano ronin spoke very loud. He looked at me and then shook his head and walked away.

Toward evening hunger made everyone quiet and finally my master spoke. He talked first of the duty of a samurai toward his lord, his master's house. How important it was that the name Asano should not be removed from the roll of the nobles of the country. "If we attack Kira before the fate of the house of Asano has been decided, then we have not been loyal but merely indulged in revenge for the sake of revenge. The deed will have been done not out of loyalty but out of vanity and pride."

Someone said (I do not know who), "But if the Asano family is given back title and domain, what happens then? Will Kira go unpunished?"

Someone else shouted, "Yes, what if Daigaku-sama is appointed heir to our late Lord, what then?"

Oishi-sama's voice remained as steady as if he were merely talking about something totally unimportant. "Restoration of the house of Asano is one thing, and revenge something else. We cannot attack Kira if our Lord's family is restored; yet the enemy of our Lord, who caused his death, must not be left untouched. If that should happen, I shall avenge the crime alone, on behalf of all of you."

"No!" several voices shouted. Then Hara Soemon asked

to be heard. Hara-sama was much older than my master, and he was much respected, even by the younger samurai.

"We have signed in our blood that we would avenge the insult to our Lord, to our clan. If you alone should take revenge, the rest of us would be deemed cowards unworthy to be called samurai. Lord Asano was lord not only to you, but to all his retainers. One cannot live under the same sky with the murderer of one's father or one's Lord. That is a saying that no one doubts. I do not know what the rest of you think, but for my part, give me a chance to attack or give me death."

I was surprised at Hara-sama; he had spoken like one of the young men. His words were followed by great shouts of agreement. I left my place by the door and went outside again to make sure that no one was listening. I had heard a little too often about that sky which you could not live under, to be moved by it. I looked up at it; it was clear and light blue, not a cloud was to be seen. Since I did not know who was my father, I might very well be living under the same sky as his murderer, that is, if he had been murdered. I walked over to the little pond; in the shadow of the rock the great carp stood immobile in the water. I nodded to it as one nods to an old friend and then went back to my post by the door.

My master was speaking again. I wondered that he could keep his voice so calm. "I am deeply moved by your faithfulness, and I have no wish other than to share your fate. I wish for Kira's death as fervently as you, but I want to wait to hear the Shogun's decision about the house of Asano. Soon it will be a year since our Lord was forced to commit seppuku; then we should be informed of the government's decision. If the decision goes against us or we do not hear, then we shall attack our enemy and satisfy the just resentment of our Lord, by cutting off Kira's head. I desire you all to trust me and let me fix the date and lead the battle."

When my master had ceased speaking there was silence for a while, then Otaka-sama spoke, agreeing that my master should be their leader and that they would trust him. They signed their names using not ink but their own blood. Then my master gave money to those of the young ones who were in need of it, and the meeting was over. That night as I laid out the bedding for my master I noticed that he looked very tired. I asked him if he wanted me to warm some sake for him. He shook his head, but then suddenly changed his mind. "Yes, Jiro, bring me a small pitcher of sake."

I hurried to the kitchen, warmed the sake, and then brought it back. I was about to leave when my master beckoned for me to stay. As he drank the rice wine he smiled. "What a marvelous plant rice is, Jiro, it gives us both food and drink. You have seen no strangers around?"

"No one. I watched most carefully, and I am sure that none overheard what happened here."

"Only you." Oishi-sama looked at me and smiled. "What you heard I shan't ask you to forget, for that would be foolish. I only ask you to keep it locked in your head, and not to spill out through your mouth what went in through your ears."

"I shan't, Oishi-sama." I bowed my head. My master said no more and I left.

·19·

Otaka Gengo
Loses His Temper

A few days after our return to Yamashina, Oishi-sama's wife sent me on an errand. As we had not been bothered by spies from Kira for some time, I was not as alert as I should have been. It was a fine day, and the sun had finally gained enough power not only to warm me thoroughly but to warm the buds on the boughs of the cherry trees enough for some of them to burst into flowers. I was standing gazing at a particularly beautiful branch of pink and white flowers, when suddenly a voice near me said, "So short is their bloom. Then their petals fall and they mix with the earth and disappear."

I turned to see who had spoken. Two samurai stood watching me. I immediately fell on my knees and bowing my head said, "That is true, my lord, but each year new flowers bloom."

"True, boy, each time a man dies a child is born screaming lustily, 'I am alive.' But that does not leave the dead less dead. Are you one of the little thieves that infest this place?"

"I am but a foolish boy, a servant of no importance," I quickly muttered. The samurai smiled and turned to his companion, who was scowling at me.

"If that boy was caught trying to steal my purse, it would then be but an act of justice to cut off his head."

"I am sure he is a little thief." The other samurai had stopped scowling and was grinning maliciously.

"I think so, too." The samurai who had been suggesting that I should lose my head drew his sword a little out off its scabbard so its steel shone in the sunlight.

"I am only a servant boy sent on an errand by my master's wife. If I do not come back they will be wondering what has happened to me."

"And who is your master?" The samurai pushed his sword back into its sheath.

"Oishi-sama! He was chief of the samurai of Lord Asano of Ako," I answered. I knew well enough that my master's name was no secret to them.

"Oh yes, we have heard of him, haven't we?" He turned to his friend. "He is a fat old man with a wart on his nose."

"Worse than that." His companion sneered. "They tell me he is not a man at all, but an old woman dressed up as one."

I said nothing but looked down upon the ground when I suddenly heard someone coughing. I looked up and saw Otaka-sama standing near, his hand resting on the hilt of his sword, contemplating the two samurai. The three men stood long, staring at each other. It seemed to me to last forever; then suddenly the samurai who had been doing most of the talking shrugged his shoulders and walked away; his friend hurried after him.

"Jiro, what strange company you keep. I don't think I approve of it. Wasps like that can sting, Jiro."

"They don't seem eager to sting now," I said, glancing at the hilt of Otaka-sama's sword.

"They were lucky, this time." Otaka Gengo drew out the sword a little and I saw he was still unarmed, wearing only the wooden one.

"Would they have killed me?" I asked, looking up at my friend who had saved me.

Otaka Gengo frowned as he considered his answer to my question, and finally he said, "Yes, I think they would have. It would have been an insult and a warning to your master. Lucky for them that I was not wearing my sword."

"What would you have done if they had drawn their swords?" I asked, getting up from my kneeling position.

"I would have thrown this into the face of the talkative one." Otaka-sama, whose left hand had been hidden behind his back, now brought it forth and let a big stone it held drop to the ground. "But I think there was little danger of it. If those two had fought me and killed me, they would not have left Yamashina alive, and they knew that well enough. Besides, such a killing would have brought trouble to Kira, the kind of trouble he has no heart for."

But they could have killed me, and that would have brought no trouble, I thought, while I said, "Thank you, my lord, for saving me."

"It was nothing. I am always glad to oblige." Otaka Gengo laughed. "I should like to be able to live to see you, Jiro, the merchant king of Osaka . . . Clad in silk and with a wife, a dozen children, and as many concubines. Now let us go and report it to your master."

Oishi-sama was furious at the news. As I had not accomplished my errand, Matsu was sent instead. Turning to Otaka-sama, my master complimented him upon keeping his temper and not fighting. He drew out his sword a little to show that it was the wooden one he was wearing.

At this my master smiled and I was ordered to the kitchen to tell the maids to bring sake. No sooner had the sake come and been poured than Matsu returned. He, too, had met the samurai. He was holding his right ear, and blood was running down his arm and flowing in a stream from his elbow. He kept saying, "I didn't insult them," repeating the words over and over again as if he needed to convince his master of his innocence. Half of his right ear had been cut off.

A maid was sent for a doctor. The cut bled a lot, but it was not dangerous. Suddenly my master looked for Otaka-sama, who had disappeared. "Jiro! Go and find him, hurry! Tell him to let them be, we don't want any trouble," he shouted.

I looked in the garden first, then decided that he probably had returned to his room in the temple on the hill above our house. I was on my way there when I saw a Buddhist monk come running. He carried a large bamboo cudgel in his hand and was wearing a wide-brimmed straw hat that hid his face. Priests and monks seldom run and this monk's stride was suspicious. I ran after him and, out of breath, finally caught up with him. Just as I suspected, it was Otaka-sama disguised as a monk.

"Oishi-sama told me to tell you to let them be," I panted, trying to keep up with him.

"And who would Oishi-sama be? I am but a poor monk

serving Buddha. There are two rascals who I want to give a lesson in humility to." Otaka-sama stopped, looked at me, and asked, "Jiro, where do you think they are?"

I told him what my errand had been and that it might be wise to look in that direction. It was an area where there were some stalls selling vegetables. As we could find them nowhere, I asked one of the stall owners if he had seen them. He nodded and pointed with his head in the direction of a small house that served as a tavern for the people of the marketplace.

"They are in there," I said, pointing to the house, and added, "but Oishi-sama said that you were to do nothing."

"Namu Amida Butsu," Otaka Gengo started to chant as he strode toward the inn. I held my breath, watching him slide open the door of the place with such force that it fell on the street. A moment later a few people came running out, followed by the fat owner of the establishment. She was in such a hurry that she stumbled in her kimono and fell on her face. She did not stay down long but scrambled away on all fours before she rose. Next came the samurai who had suggested that I should lose my head. He came flying out as if someone had kicked him and a moment later his companion followed, holding the side of his head. He, too, now had lost an ear! Last of all came Otaka Gengo, with one of the samurai's swords in his hand. He looked around for his enemies, but they had fled. Glancing at the spectators that had collected, he threw the sword away and put his hands in the position of prayer. "Namu Amida Butsu," he chanted in a resounding voice, and then strode off. I followed, having no desire to stay and meet his victims again.

"Now remember, Jiro" — Otaka-sama turned to me as we came to the gate of our house — "you don't know the monk who did it. He must have been some traveling holy man." Otaka-sama winked and then ran up to the temple.

"Did you find him?" Oishi-sama asked as soon as he saw me. "Did you tell him what I said?"

"Yes," I said. "I told him."

"He has a terrible temper, but he is a good man." Oishi-sama nodded to emphasize what he had said.

"Yes," I agreed and went to look for Matsu to find out how he was.

·20·

My Master Is Divorced

"Your master, Jiro, is a true samurai. He is like Benkei, the perfect retainer. What am I?" Otaka-sama sighed. "That joke with the dog was more foolish than funny and then attacking the two Kira samurai. The whole idea is to make Kira believe that he is safe, that we don't care what happened to our Lord, and that we have no thought of revenge, and what do I do . . ." Again Otaka-sama sighed and shook his head. "Is your master angry with me? I have not dared come to see him."

"I am glad you cut the ear of that fellow," I said. We were sitting in the garden in a spot that could not be seen from the house. Below us in the valley travelers were hastening by on the road to Kyoto. "Oishi-sama is angry and not angry. I had to tell him several times what happened and when I described how you cleared out the sake shop he smiled, but then he frowned."

"It's my temper, I just can't control it. A true samurai must always be mastering himself, as a rider should be one with his horse and therefore in control of it. But I'm not like that; I get angry and show it or I think of something funny and I laugh without giving a thought to my dignity. Dignity is very important, don't you think?"

"I don't have any, so I have never thought about it. But I suppose to a samurai it is important." Now I pondered it for a moment. "Sometimes though, dignity is used only to hide that you are of no importance."

"What do you mean?" Otaka-sama frowned, looking at me.

"If a samurai tells you that he is going to kill you because your shadow has fallen upon him or you have gotten in his way by mistake . . ." I wasn't exactly sure of what I was saying, though I knew what I meant.

"That's not dignity." Otaka Gengo shook his head. "That's just foolishness."

"I know," I said. "But still that is the form of 'dignity' you meet often as a servant. I'm not sure I know what dignity is, but you're right, Oishi-sama has dignity if there is such a thing." I had gotten used to being able to say almost anything I felt like to Otaka-sama.

"Dignity!" Otaka-sama pronounced the word carefully and then paused to contemplate it, finally shaking his head and grinning. "Jiro, I must forget about it. I will never become dignified, yet I would like to be. That is strange, Jiro. I have great ability with my sword, my arrows seldom fail to hit the target, and there are few horses in Japan that I cannot master. Yet I think nothing of all these accomplishments merely because I can do them. But the one thing I cannot do, be dignified, I hold to be greater than all the others." Otaka-sama laughed. "Tell me, Jiro, what is happening in the house?" He asked and nodded toward it.

"My master is divorcing his wife and she is to go to her brother and take the three younger children with her. She is very sad, and her eyes are seldom without tears. I feel very sorry for her."

"But Jiro, that is for the best. It is to protect his wife that he is doing it. Once we have avenged our Lord and killed Kira, the Shogun might punish our families as well. I have no wife and children. If I had I would do the same. I have only a mother; my father has long been dead." Otaka-sama smiled. "You cannot divorce a mother, or I would, to protect her for she has been good to me. Still the Shogun — even Inu-kubo — won't hurt her, I hope."

I rose. I could hear my mother calling me. I bowed toward Otaka-sama, for though we were friends he was also far above me.

"Tell me, Jiro, if your master mentions me," Otaka-sama demanded. "And when it is safe for me to come for a visit."

I nodded and ran to the house. Turning to look back once I saw that the samurai was picking burrs from the coat of the dog.

A week after that conversation, my master's wife and three of his children left the house forever. Chikara, too, left, but he was to return after he had seen his mother to his uncle's residence. My master had given him the choice of staying or leaving. Chikara had not even paused to breathe, but had immediately said he would follow his father even to the world beyond. He had bragged about it to me, though by now he treated me more as a servant than a friend.

Matsu and two of the young women who served my

master's wife left with her. I was sorry to see Matsu go. He had always been kind to me. His ear was still bandaged, and he was so frightened that I don't think he had left the house since his wound. He was a good servant, for he had no wish to be or become anything else; he had accepted his status without difficulty. I wasn't so lucky.

All that was left of servants in the house were my mother, a girl not much older than I was, and me, Jiro. My mother was happy; she would now be in charge, or at least she thought she would. My master never took an interest in the household. He would not notice if the house became dirty. As for the food, though my mother was not a good cook, she was a big eater. The quality of our meals might not be great, but there would be plenty of food.

My master had accompanied his wife on the first day's journey, telling us he would return the next day. That night my mother cooked a good meal for the three of us, consisting of the leftovers from the night before when my master and his wife had supped unusually well. My mother's face was red and I guessed that she had been at the sake. She did not drink while she ate, but in the middle of the meal she excused herself and went over to the cooking place, pretending to look at the charcoal fire. I noticed that a cup was near it and that she drank from it and obviously emptied it. When she returned she was in great humor.

"Jiro, I dreamed last night that I was a fish," she declared and laughed. "I swam around and around, then suddenly the water disappeared and I became myself again. Was that a good or a bad omen?"

"If you didn't bite on a hook and get caught, I suppose

it is not a bad one." Oishi-sama would not notice if she drank his sake, but I didn't like it.

"I wonder if the water disappearing could be the old lady leaving." My mother wrinkled her brow, then suddenly grinned, pleased with herself and the state of the world.

"I dreamed that I was getting married," the little servant girl suddenly said. I looked surprised at her for she seldom spoke. She was a frightened little thing and had been nicknamed Usagi, rabbit. I suppose she had a real name, but I had never heard it.

"Who would marry you?" my mother asked in disgust and waddled over to where she had kept her sake cup and a little sake pitcher. Deciding not to hide them she brought both over to the table we were sitting at. As she sank down on the floor beside me, she said, "Maybe you were marrying Jiro in your dream."

"Oh, no!" the little girl exclaimed. "He was very handsome, and wore a silk kimono."

My mother laughingly took hold of my kimono and fingered the cloth as if she were examining it. "No, it isn't silk," she finally said and then, scrutinizing my face, declared, "and he isn't handsome."

Usagi, finally realizing that she might have hurt my feelings, said in a voice near tears, "But it was only a silly dream. I know no one will marry me." Then looking at me she whispered, "You're not ugly."

I had had enough of this discussion about my looks. I rose, nodded to the girl to show that I wasn't angry at her, and then with, I hoped, a very sour expression on my face I bowed to my mother and left. The moon had risen above the treetops; from the temple I heard the sound of a flute. I knew that Otaka Gengo played that instrument and that he had a room there. I thought of going up there and took a few steps in that direction. The flute player stopped his music, and a bat flew silently by. The sudden stillness of the night made me pause. Suddenly I felt so miserable that I could have cried, but no tears came. I went back to the house and found that my mother had already gone to sleep. The little girl was cleaning up. When she saw me she smiled timidly, and I smiled back at her to reassure her. I sat down by the table, which now had been cleared, and stared at the girl who was washing the dishes in a bowl. I thought, *It is true, Jiro, you are not handsome or clever. You are nothing at all.*

I Get a Room of My Own

"Jiro!" Oishi-sama looked at me and smiled. "You shall be staying up late from now on."

I nodded as if I understood what he meant, which I didn't. But a servant always agrees with his master, even if he is promised a beating.

"You shall be my moon, my guiding light in the floating world. When good men sleep, the floating world wakes up. I have a lantern made for you to carry. When it is dark you shall walk in front of me. The paper lantern will have my crest on it, for I want everyone to know who I am. In the floating world many people do not wear their crests on their kimono and certainly not on a lamp . . ." My master stopped talking and looked away for so long that for a moment I almost thought that he had forgotten me. "It is necessary that your master becomes one of the twigs that float in that world. We shall visit the kind of houses where more sake than tea is drunk. Often I shall appear late at night as if I needed a young shoulder to lean upon. As for dignity, I shall leave that here at home. Your duty will be to carry the lantern and to tell anyone who asks you that your master has become addicted to sake and the company of samisen-strumming ladies. Your duty will also be to keep your eyes and ears open and to tell me what they have seen or heard. Do you understand me?"

"Yes, master. I am to carry a lantern for you when you go out at night."

"Yes, Jiro, a lantern . . . Has Otaka Gengo not come here? I have not seen him since he played the barber to Kira's men."

"He is very sorry for what he did. He is afraid that you are angry with him."

"And how do you know that?" my master asked.

"He told me so." I bowed my head.

"He should not tell you that. He lacks decorum, he does not always behave as a samurai should." Oishi-sama frowned.

"Sometimes even a great lord who rules a large district might, when he is alone, talk to his horse or his falcon," I said, crestfallen.

"That is true, but the difference between a servant and a horse or falcon is that the latter can't talk back." Suddenly my master laughed. "You are a clever boy, Jiro, and that is why I have kept you here. Matsu would not do; he is loyal but too full of fear. I asked him before he left to find clothes for you, suitable for a servant. I do not want you to shame me. They are lying in the room he used, and you may sleep there now. He thought they would fit you; if not, have the girl change them. She can sew; she is to look after our clothes and wash them."

I rose and was just about to leave when my master called me back. "You may tell Otaka Gengo that I should like

him to come in the morning to drink a cup of tea with
me."

I went straight to the closet-like room that had been
Matsu's, and there, folded neatly, were some clothes —
two cotton kimonos and a warm jacket as well. Beside them
lay a new pair of straw sandals and on top of the clothes a
dark blue obi. I tried one of the kimonos on; it fitted me,
as did the jacket. A servant tucks up his kimono, so he can
run to do his master's bidding. A samurai never runs once
he has grown his topknot. For a moment I thought of
wearing my new clothes, but decided against it. I put on
my old clothes which, though clean, had been repaired in
several places, and that not very expertly. A room of my
own — I looked around the tiny cubicle — if I stretched
out my arms my hands could almost reach its walls in all
directions. Still it was a place I could call my own. I had
always slept next to my mother since I could remember,
usually on the kitchen floor.

My mother was far from pleased when I told her what
had happened and that I had been given Matsu's room. First
she snorted in contempt, then she called me Jiro-sama. I
knelt and bowed to her and declared that it was by no wish
of my own but by our master's order that I was to move to
Matsu's room. I further said, which was untrue, that I had
no wish to sleep anywhere but next to her and ended up
declaring that I was a worthless son.

This mollified my mother a little, and she heartily agreed
about my worthlessness, declaring that I was a disreputable
urchin whose head no doubt, in good time, would be exhibited on the execution grounds. As for my carrying a lantern
for our master, she doubted that I would be capable of this

without setting the town on fire. Then she turned her back, saying that she was too busy to waste her time talking to me, though I couldn't see that she was doing anything at all beyond drinking a cup of tea.

Otaka-sama's room was in a small pavilion in back of the temple. A light was burning inside but I could hear nothing. I knew he was there, for you never leave a room with a candle burning. "Otaka-sama," I called.

"Who's there?" Otaka-sama asked, sounding annoyed at being disturbed.

"It's me," I answered foolishly.

"Me? Now who could that possibly be? A Tengu who has come down from the mountains to greet me? How long is your nose? If it is over a foot long then you are a Tengu. Or maybe you are a fox in disguise?"

"It's me, Jiro," I answered.

"So that's who me is. Well, come in, me." Now Otaka-sama was laughing.

I slid the door open, hurried inside, and then closed it behind me. Kneeling, I said, "Oishi-sama has sent me to ask you to come in the morning and drink tea with him."

"That is kind of him. You may tell him that I shall be pleased to." Otaka-sama was holding a brush in his hand. On a low table in front of him were paper and an inkstone. I looked at what he had written but I couldn't read it. "It is a poem," the samurai said and read it aloud:

So silent is the night
That I can hear my heart beat,
The wind has gone to sleep.

I said nothing but nodded. Otaka-sama frowned. "Jiro, you must learn to read and to write, or you will never become a rich Osaka merchant clad in silk."

"I would like to very much," I said and meant it. Then I asked, "Why does one write poems?"

Otaka-sama smiled good-naturedly. "Now that is a very good question, Jiro. Some do, I think, because others do it; that is mere foolishness. Monkeys aping their masters. Others out of loneliness, and some because they are in love. A poem is a painting of a thought. No" — the samurai shook his head — "it is not a painting, even though it has been put down with a brush, and it is not a thought either as much as a mood caught and made permanent, imprisoned on a piece of paper."

I nodded again, though I was far from sure that I had understood what Otaka-sama meant.

"Jiro, I think your head is very loosely attached to your neck for it seems to me that you are always nodding. There is a youngster here who is a little older than you. He is an acolyte going to become a priest, and he shall teach you."

"I cannot pay him," I said, thinking, *I must learn not to nod so much.*

"He will do it for very little, and I shall take care of that. Tell me, is your master still angry at me?"

"I don't think so anymore. But he is very concerned that Kira's spies should tell their master that he has no plan of revenge."

"I know." Otaka-sama frowned. "That earless one will go back to Edo and tell Kira a tall story. It was foolish of me." The samurai shook his head in despair, but then suddenly he smiled. "We are what we are, Jiro. It's hard to change yourself. I shall keep tight reins on that temper of mine; be sure of that. I'm sorry for what I did. But I'm not sorry that he lost an ear; I only wish I had cut off both of them." He took another piece of paper, dipped his brush in ink and wrote something on it, then contemplated it, and read it aloud. " 'The fish in the pond has reached a great age, but gained little wisdom.' That is me, Jiro, short on wisdom. Tell your master that I shall await eagerly for the sun to rise."

I was just about to nod, but instead I said that I would and bowed as I left. When I came outside the wind had woken up and I could hear it moan in the treetops.

·22·

The Floating World

"The floating world." A strange name. A world not solid as the ramparts of the Shogun's castle in Edo. For the stones in those walls are made of ambitions, the wish to power, the wish to rule. The bamboo walls of the floating world are built of dreams as fragile as the morning mist. Many who have entered the floating world have sunk into it and disappeared. To be of importance in that world one needs not a famous name, or a well-known crest on one's kimono; one needs only money, silver, or, best of all, gold. It is a world for sale, and yet when it has been bought it is not yours. Maybe that is its attraction, an attempt to make a dream real, to dream while awake. To make solid what is not solid, to end desire by fulfilling it. A fools' heaven, but often visited by men who are wise.

Our first visit to that world took place in a district of Kyoto called Shimabara. It was not dark yet, and I had not lit my lantern, but my master insisted on my walking a few steps ahead of Otaka Gengo and himself, as if I were leading them. He ordered me to stop at a certain house, which I did. My master and his friend stood for a moment contemplating the building.

"They say that everything here is of the very best quality, the sake as well as the women." Suddenly one could hear the brittle tones coming from someone playing the samisen. A woman's voice sang a song that I had never heard sung so beautifully before. I looked at Otaka-sama. He, too, had been moved by the tenderness of the voice. "I believe it," he mumbled. "If her face is as charming as her voice, she must be a great beauty."

"Let us enter and see." My master moved toward the door of the house. A man who had been loitering nearby opened it for him and bowed. My master took a copper coin from his sleeve and gave it to him. Then, turning to me — I thought he had forgotten my existence — he said, "Jiro, you are to wait here for us. When it grows dark you can light the lantern. Here!" He threw me a copper coin, which fell in the street, and I picked it up. By the time I had done this, they had disappeared and the door to the house was closed.

"Who is your master?" the man who had opened the door asked, looking me over carefully.

"Oishi Kuranosuke, chief retainer of Lord Asano of Ako," I answered and bowed just enough for politeness' sake.

"I have heard of him." The man gave a barely noticeable nod, to indicate that he had observed my greeting. "He is masterless. Lord Asano committed seppuku more than a year ago."

"That is true," I said. "But we have not heard yet if Lord Asano's brother is to keep his title. Until then I do not think my master considers himself masterless."

The man made a face as if to say, it doesn't matter, so

long as he has money to spend. "Wait across the street, not in front of the door. If your master comes I shall call you."

Now began a long vigil. At first I was alone keeping watch, but soon other customers of the teahouse arrived with servants who, like me, were told to wait for their masters. None was as young as I, and most of them knew each other. They talked freely of their masters' business, some bragging, and some censuring it. Their masters seemed not to be samurai, but merchants of one kind or another. Most of them were men in their prime, and carried not only lanterns to light their master's steps, but stout canes as well. I realized that they were there as guards against attack by robbers, as well as lantern carriers. Finally one of them deigned to notice me, and asked who my master was. I repeated what I had told the guard at the teahouse. This time it was greeted by laughter.

"A ronin, who, when he has spent his master's money, will come creeping to ours to ask for a job loading ships," one of the older men said and sniffed as if he had smelled something unpleasant.

"No, no," another objected. "He is a valiant fellow; they say he is going to avenge his master." The speaker looked at me kindly for a moment. "They say that before the year is over the hatamoto that caused his master's disgrace will be dead."

"He is avenging his master in there." The speaker nodded toward the teahouse. "By spending his gold or whatever he took with him out of Ako castle. I say the man is nothing but a thief! I say that the Shogun's men found the castle bare when they went in."

I don't know why I wanted to defend Oishi-sama, for in

truth the picture of my master the last speaker had drawn was one he would have approved of, since it would put his enemy Kira at ease. "Why don't you tell him that when he comes out?" I finally said instead of agreeing with him, which I should have done, according to my master's instruction.

"Yes, tell him to his face that he is nothing but a thief." The man who had called my master valiant spoke with passion. I looked at him and thought, *He could be a ronin who has been forced to sell his swords. Or he could have been once in the service of a samurai of some standing, and recalling that regrets that he is now serving a merchant.*

"If I told all two-sword men what I thought of them, I would soon be a head shorter," the other grumbled while the rest of the servants laughed and agreed with him. "But as for youngsters who still have their mother's milk on their lips, I will take no insolence from them, or I shall teach them good manners," he said, glowering at me.

"Let the boy be," said the oldest of the servants, looking kindly at me. "That a servant defends the master who fills his rice bowl is as it should be."

"Which means that our true masters are our stomachs. Whoever fills them we bow to." The man I suspected of once having been a samurai grinned as he said this. "Our loyalty depends upon the state of our stomachs; if they are empty so is our loyalty. But maybe that is true for the samurai as well, only their rice bowls or stomachs are larger than ours."

"In our house there is more millet than rice in the bowls," one of the servants grudgingly said, which made the others laugh.

"Come." The servant who had defended my master beckoned to me and I followed him. In the back of the teahouse was an entrance to what I believed was the kitchen, at least the smell told me so. He entered but told me to wait. A moment later he was back. "Your master and his friend have just ordered food and more sake; mine too is busy enjoying himself. I will take you to someplace where we can get something to eat, I suppose you are too young to drink anything more potent than tea."

I nodded, for though I had tasted sake, I didn't care much for it. Down a narrow lane we came to a house that catered to servants, or to any riffraff that possessed a copper coin or two. The place was crowded and very noisy, and we found a corner and sat down on the floor next to a low table.

"The owner is the same, but the service is not. Though some of these women" — he nodded toward one of the waitresses — "have once served in the other house."

"You mean the same man owns this place as the one where Oishi-sama is?" I asked, surprised.

"Or the same woman. There was a man once, I think, but he is long dead. The old witch has a son but he is of little use to her, or to himself."

A woman came over to us and my newfound friend gave an order, then he said something which I didn't understand, but it made the woman laugh. She was just about to go, when he told her to wait and then asked my name. When I told him he said, "Jiro here is a friend of mine. Take good care of him. His master used to serve my master. Jiro" — he glanced at me — "this is Kamoko, she is the most honest woman in Shimabara, which does not mean much, I agree. But she likes young boys."

The woman laughed and looked me over for a minute. Then she leaned over and, touching the scar on my forehead, said, "I will put my mark on him." And she walked away.

My friend followed her with his eyes. "She is kind and honest. If you ever find yourself hungry without any money in your purse, she will feed you."

"Why is she called Kamoko?" I asked. It meant a little duck.

"She waddles like one," my friend said. "And she is getting as fat as one."

"You said that you served my master's master. Did you serve Lord Asano?" I asked.

"I was born in Ako, and my father was a servant in his castle. I suppose one can say that I served him, insofar as the child of a servant serves his father's master. But I ran away as soon as hair started to grow on my chin. It was more to my taste to bow and scrape in Kyoto than in Ako."

"Whom do you serve?" I asked.

"A man who sells everything. If there was money to be earned by it, he would sell you as well. Mostly it is silk, which he gets from Kai. Oh, he is wonderfully clever, but a bit of a fool as well. He throws his money about, but precious little ends up in my sleeve." My friend sighed, but then, as Kamoko came with our food and a pitcher of sake for him, he laughed and rubbed his stomach.

The food was the best I had ever eaten. I gave him my copper coin besides another that I had in my sleeve, but he waved them away. "I have money, Jiro, and one of these days when I have enough I shall become a merchant myself.

Here in Shimabara money is the true God, the only God, and we all worship and hate it."

After two more pitchers of sake, and after I had drunk many cups of tea, a young girl my own age came. She beckoned to us from across the room. My friend rose. "Either your master or mine is getting ready to leave. We'd better go back." The merchant's servant was also carrying a lantern. As he paid, Kamoko lit them for us. She noticed the crest on mine and frowned, but did not say anything.

"Did you notice the old hag that I paid to, Jiro? She is called Bones, for she is as thin as a skeleton, but she's sharp. She and the woman who owns the place are very close, and the owner is as fat as she is thin."

"What is the owner called?" I asked, expecting it to be "lard" or "fat."

"She — I'm not sure, the girls call her Mother, I'm not even sure they know her name. She owns more than these two houses." We had come back to the house. "She is like a spider in the middle of the net, fat on all the flies it has caught."

It was not my master but my newfound friend's master who had decided to leave. He was a stout man in the middle of his life. My friend bowed humbly as he saw him and then walked off in front of him. I had to wait long before my master came. The moon had moved across the sky and set before the two samurai came out.

Otaka Gengo greeted me; Oishi-sama merely muttered, "Home" and we set out, I leading with my little lantern. The sky in the east was already growing light before we reached our house, and so passed my first night in the floating world.

·23·

Chikamatsu Monzaemon

"And how are you enjoying the floating world? Are you swimming or floating in it or are you drowning?" Otaka-sama smiled, though he managed at the same time to look unhappy. Since our first visit to the teahouse, my master had made many more, but Otaka-sama seldom accompanied him, and I sensed that the samurai did not approve of my master's appearance in such company.

"I'm not swimming, on the other hand I'm not in danger of drowning, so I guess I'm floating," I said. My master was still asleep after a long night of drinking, and I had walked up to the temple. It was now midsummer and the days were getting very hot and humid, for the climate of Kyoto is not of the best — too hot in summer and too cold in winter.

"I like sake as well as any other man, even a cup too much at times. But to carry on like that practically every night, it surprises me." Otaka-sama sighed.

"Well, it's to fool Kira, to make him think that my master has drowned in that world, or is going to." Though we were sitting in the shade of a great pine tree I could feel the sweat running down my body and the dry kimono I had put on that morning was already wet.

"Are you sure, Jiro? Are you certain that Oishi has not taken a liking to it? I have heard that he stays with one of the women there. Is that true?"

I nodded. "I think so. Her name is O'Karu and she is very beautiful, or so I have been told. I haven't seen her. I have only heard about it, but everybody is very jealous of his luck."

"Has Chikara heard about it as well?" Otaka Gengo shook his head.

"Yes, I think he knows, but my master has refused to take him along, which has made him very angry. He walks around the house like a black cloud and won't speak to anyone."

"We are attracted to that world like bees to the flowers where they suck their honey. But I don't trust it, for it changes you."

"I don't think it has changed my master. He will appear as drunk as you can be, when he leaves the house, hardly able to walk. Once he even leaned on me. But as soon as we are well away he stands as straight and walks as freely as if he has drunk nothing but tea. It is only a ruse, but I wish Chikara would think so as well." I felt sure that what I said was true and that my master had not changed.

"Maybe what I meant is that I fear the floating world because I am afraid it can change me." Otaka-sama smiled and then lightheartedly said, "But has it changed you, Jiro?"

"I know only the outside of that world; I have seen the kitchen where the food is cooked, not the rooms where the music is played."

"One day, Jiro, the time of the samurai will be over. I'm not sure it isn't already, and we just don't know it. I've always thought that Oishi Kuranosuke is the true last samurai; maybe that is why I hate to watch what he is doing to himself. There must be something that is not for sale, that cannot be bought or bartered. Something that is so precious that it has no price. Do you understand what I mean? Oh, you're just a child." Otaka-sama turned away from me in disgust.

"I'm sorry," I muttered, for indeed I was. I understood what he meant but how could I share it?

"Oh, I forget how young you are, but that is because you are such a clever boy." Then, as if he had suddenly realized why I could not "understand" him, he said, "And you are not a samurai, I know, I know."

"We are going to that same house where we went the first night. We have gone to many other places as well — a week ago we went as far as Osaka. I think Oishi-sama wanted to see someone there."

"Has he ever asked for me to come?" Otaka-sama looked away.

"Only yesterday he was wondering what you were doing and why you never came." This was true, but I thought that my master had guessed why Otaka Gengo kept away, and that it was a sign of disapproval. "He is sleeping now for he was very tired."

"Tell him when he wakes that I will join him tonight." Otaka-sama rose. His dog, which was lying nearby, opened one eye, but closed it again. It was too hot to move. I walked back to our house and to my room to lie down and try to sleep. The air in my tiny room was heavy and still with the heat.

It was late in the afternoon, and I was ready to accompany my master to the floating world of Kyoto. It was cooler now, more bearable. I was getting my little lantern ready in the kitchen when Chikara burst in.

"My father has promised that I can come, too." My master's son looked proudly at me. "Are the women very beautiful, Jiro?"

"I have been told so, but I have not been inside the houses that your father frequents." This was true, though I had actually seen some of them. One had been very beautiful indeed, the others I had thought merely pretty.

"It is only a ruse to fool Kira." Chikara tried to look as adult as he could, but like his father he was not tall and he looked very young for his sixteen years.

"I know," I said. "A servant of a samurai tried to befriend me the other day. His master was in the house watching your father, spying on him. He would not tell me the name of the samurai he served or what clan he belonged to, but I'm sure he was one of Kira's men."

"What did you tell him?"

"What your father told me to say." I smiled. "That Oishi-sama has decided that there are only two things that are important in this world, sake and women, and in that order, too."

"But it is only a ruse," Chikara repeated, looking unhappily at me. "To fool Kira," he added lamely.

He's not absolutely sure that it's true, I thought, and felt sorry for the boy who worshiped his father.

"I must go and dress in my best kimono." Chikara frowned then smiled as he thought of the night. "I, too, like my father can drink sake."

The sun was low in the horizon when we set out for Kyoto. Otaka-sama had come, as he promised. When we arrived at the teahouse, my master handed me some copper coins and said, "It might be late, Jiro, but still before the moon sets be back here and wait for us." The guard at the teahouse had slid open the door and was bowing deeply, for my master was known to be free with his money. It was the first time that Oishi-sama had told me when I could expect him to leave. I wondered if that was because Chikara was along. He and Otaka-sama were waiting for my master to enter first.

I bowed almost as deeply as the doorkeeper had and did not raise my head before I heard the door being closed.

"He is a good master; there are few of them who care if their servants go hungry," the guard declared. "Few of our customers are more popular than he is. Who was the young one with him?"

"His son," I said. "It is the first time his father has taken him along." I was looking down the street and wondering where I should go myself.

"The teachers here know how to instruct such young ones. They will teach him what life is about," the guard said with a sneer. I nodded and walked away. I had never liked the man. He claimed that he had once worn the two swords, but I doubted it. He was one of the rats in the floating world, living on and off the trash found there.

I decided that I was hungry enough to eat. I did not go to the place where I had gone the first time that I had accompanied my master. Instead, I went to a small soba shop run by an old woman who claimed that she had once been the most beautiful woman in Shimabara. A Tayu, the highest rank among the women of the floating world. Whether this was true or not, I could well believe it, for she had the manners of a woman who was used to being obeyed. Because she had taken a liking to me, she would tell me stories from her youth. Her cook was an old woman, too, who had been her servant all her life. The menu was simple, only noodle dishes, but they are my favorite food.

The soba shop was tiny, containing only three tables. The kitchen in back was open so you could watch your food being prepared. It was clean and in the entrance there was space for the straw sandals and getas of her guests. Since none of the tables was free I asked permission to seat myself at one occupied by only two customers. One of them nodded his permission, while the other just continued eating without paying any attention to me.

I ordered a double portion of cold buckwheat noodles, and leaned back against the wall, stretching out my legs. The tatami floor was newly swept. I was wondering if the two women slept there, or if they lived in another place, when one of the men at my table said, "He was a poor Yoshitsune; he acted as if a mouse might have frightened him."

The other man smiled and nodded and said, "But he's handsome; notice that the theater was full. So many women had begged their husbands to take them."

"Yes." The other man laughed. "Many a woman in

Kyoto will dream tonight that it is he who is lying beside them rather than their fat-bellied husbands." Just then someone else entered and the two actors, for such they were, greeted him with loud cries of "Monza!"

He made a courteous bow to them and sat down next to me. "Have you heard about the latest murder?" he asked and looked expectantly at his two friends. When they shook their heads he continued, "It is a wonderful story, the oilseller's wife was done in some time ago, but now they have caught her murderer. They all thought she had died for love, but it was for money he killed her. Those are the only two reasons for murder, love or money. In this case I suspect it was both — she loved him and he loved her money. It is a good story."

"An oilseller's wife and some riffraff — will that be something that anyone would care to watch?" one of the actors asked disdainfully. "Can't you find a better story than that?"

"Probably," the man called Monza replied and ordered noodles and sake. "They had a fight in the oilshop when he killed her. They struggled and upset one big jar of oil, and when they fought on, they must have been covered in oil. That would be a great thing to enact, the two of them fighting, she for her life, and he for her money, both as slippery as a couple of eels. The story is worth telling just for that scene."

My food had come. I ate it very slowly for I wanted to listen to every word that was said. It was mostly talk of the theater, where all three of them worked. They gossiped about other actors, and the owners of the theaters as well.

"I think, though, that I shall soon write only for puppets,

rather than for you." The one they called Monza laughed. "They only strut when I want them to, and as for adding lines of their own, they can't."

"The puppet theater is but a craze, it will not last," one of the actors objected. "The women of Kyoto will not fall in love with a doll."

"Perhaps not." Monza rose. "But then I don't write plays for silly women to giggle at." Suddenly, as he prepared to leave, he smiled good-naturedly at me. "Don't pay attention to them, boy; they are not real men, only ghosts in search of souls that people like me supply them with." Noticing the scar on my forehead, he ran a finger along it. "There is a story there; someday you must tell it to me." Then with a nod to his two companions he left.

"Without us, where would he be? He would have to mumble his lines to himself, like old men who have out-lived their own wits do." The man who spoke threw some coppers on the table and rose.

"He is but a scribbler, but he is the best of them," his friend said as he followed him, laughing.

Long after the door had closed behind them I could still feel the touch of Monza's finger on my brow. When I had paid for my meal I asked the owner who her customers had been.

"The two who sat at the table when you came are only a couple of riverside beggars; they are happy even if their names appear last on the billboard. The other writes the words for them. He is a clever man. He once wrote a letter for me."

"What is his name?" I asked. "I heard they called him Monza."

"It is Chikamatsu Monzaemon. He comes here sometimes. He claims he is fond of my noodles, but he is fond of sake as well, and that is a good thing for there is more profit in a sake drinker than in those who drink so much tea that one might suspect that they have a fire in their stomachs that they need to quench." She laughed and I blushed, for I had kept the little girl busy refilling my teacup.

When I came out the moon had risen, but was not in its zenith yet. I went back to the teahouse to wait. Everywhere fireflies were blinking their little lights. I remembered the man who wrote the actor's words for them and thought, *yes, I will tell him my story,* and because I made that promise I retold it to myself, and so the night passed until my master came. Oishi-sama as usual acted as if he had had too much of the sake, but Chikara did not need to act that part; twice he almost fell on our way home, which made my master and Otaka-sama laugh.

·24·

A Message from Edo

"Do you know a man who makes up the words the actors speak? I can't remember his name, but I think it ended in 'matsu.' " I looked at the young monk whom Otaka Gengo had made my teacher. I liked him, though I was fairly certain that without being paid he wouldn't have agreed to teach me.

"Sure." The young man grinned. "He comes from the same place as I do." The way the monk had talked about the town where he was born made me feel certain that he had not minded leaving it. "He had another name then. My parents knew him."

"I saw him last night down in the pleasure quarters," I said.

"Oh, so that's where he holds out." The young man sniffed virtuously. "He wanted to become a bonze, but found that the early hours and the food didn't agree with him. He worshiped Buddha in the same temple as I did, Konsho-ji in Karatsu. They still talk about him there. Some say he was so eager to leave that he swam across the strait to the big island. That may just be nonsense, but he never went back home either, and I can't blame him."

"What's wrong with your hometown?" I asked, glancing down at the paper where I had written all the forty-seven letters of the kana alphabet. Although I thought they looked very pretty, I knew my teacher would find much to criticize in them. The thought of all the Kanji, the thousands of Chinese characters, I would have to learn in order really to be able to read and write made me wish I had never said I would like to acquire that skill.

"Oh, I suppose there is nothing wrong with it, that is if you like it. It's not a big town, but it has a good harbor. Once I saw a foreign ship; it sailed close to the shore — maybe it was heading for China. Some of the fishermen have sailed over there, even though it isn't allowed. In Nagasaki foreign ships often come; they're funny looking and very big, or so I am told, I mean the sailors . . . Maybe every place is bad to some people and good to others. I liked the smell from the sea. My mother died when I was ten and my father married again."

"Oh!" I said.

The monk smiled. "You're wrong, my young friend. I never could stand my father, not even when my mother was alive. His idea of obedience from his wife or his children was the subservience of a slave. They told me that Konsho-ji was a very strict temple to serve in. I didn't find it so, because I was used to worse. Let me look at what you have written." The young man looked down at the paper and said, "You use too coarse a brush. A beginner should use a normal brush; only a master can handle a coarse one without making a mess."

When my lesson was over I bowed and thanked him, and

said that I was sorry I was such a poor student and I was probably too stupid ever to learn to write decently.

He bowed as well and said that he was sorry he was such a poor teacher and he himself was really too clumsy even to think of teaching anyone else. Then he laughed and I laughed too. As I left he said, "Jiro, for someone who has just begun you are doing very well."

When I came down to our house, I felt immediately that something of importance had taken place. I could hear Otaka Gengo and my master talking together. I went to the kitchen and asked my mother what had happened.

"Somebody came," she said and shook her head. "He did not come to see me," she added needlessly.

"Where did he come from?" I demanded.

"How should I know? But he looked tired, as if he had traveled far and had been in a hurry to do it." She frowned at me. "I don't think he had any message for you either." Then suddenly she looked grave. "But maybe he had a message for both you and me, and just forgot to deliver it."

"And what would that message be that he did not deliver?" I asked.

"That soon we will be masterless." She grinned. "A couple of ronin."

"But instead of two swords you will be wearing two wooden ladles or maybe chopsticks. Did the messenger come from Edo?" I asked.

"I think so." My mother nodded. "Two chopsticks and no rice to fetch with them."

I went in search of Chikara, hoping to learn what had happened. I didn't find him, but saw Otaka Gengo, who was just leaving. He, seeing the expression on my face, stopped long enough to tell me.

"Someone came from Edo. The Shogun has released Lord Daigaku from confinement, but banished him and the family will not be restored."

"And what does that mean?" I asked.

Otaka-sama looked a little surprised at me. "That we are free to act, Jiro. Now we can avenge our master. In times of peace the samurai has no opportunity to show his valor, but now we have been given this chance." Otaka-sama smiled. "We shall be remembered and our names shall become household words that mothers will teach their children."

I wanted to ask more questions but he walked away, striding up to the temple above where he lived. I sat down for a moment upon a favorite stone in the garden and thought the matter over. Nearly all the samurai who had made the covenant to avenge their master, and signed their names with their blood, had families. What would happen to their wives and children? I didn't understand them. I would have been like those samurai who, when the money had been divided, had immediately tried to find another master to serve. I felt ashamed at having such thoughts. I wouldn't steal from, or do anything dishonest to, my master, Oishi-sama, but I would not die for him. I shook my head in disgust and mumbled out loud, "But you, Jiro, are nothing but a servant boy and a servant boy is nothing . . ." I searched for something that I could compare myself to, but couldn't think of anything so I ended up whispering, "nothing at all."

A voice called me; it was my master's. He, too, looked as happy as if he had received good news. I was sent with a message to one of the Asano ronin in Kyoto. There was to be a meeting of the retainers who lived in Kyoto and Osaka a few days later. Otaka Gengo had left for Osaka to tell those who lived there to come. The meeting was to be held in the temple in Kyoto.

I liked being sent on errands like that because in Kyoto there was always something to see. It was a long walk; between Yamashina and Kyoto there were some low hills to climb, and by the time I reached the outskirts of the town, it was already growing dark and the first star of the evening could be found in the sky. The samurai lived in a room he had rented above a rice shop. The owner greeted me with such respect that I felt sure he was terrified of his lodger, who was one of the younger of Lord Asano's retainers. I knew him, but not well. I gave him the letter from my master, and while he read it I looked around the room where he lived. I was kneeling by the door and saw that his bedding had not been put away from the night before and the place had an air of neglect and disorder.

"Tell Oishi-sama" — as the samurai said my master's name he bowed a little — "that I shall fulfill his instructions."

I bowed my head until my brow touched the floor and then started to crawl backward out of the room. But the samurai stopped me with a movement of his hand. "When did you hear?" he asked.

"A messenger came from Edo this morning; I was away

so I do not know exactly when. Otaka-sama has gone to Osaka to tell the people there."

"Good!" the samurai exclaimed. "I was afraid that our swords would become rusty and our arms decrepit with age before anything would happen."

I nodded my agreement to this sentiment and waited to be dismissed.

"Your master is in good health?" the Ako ronin asked.

"Yes, he is well," I replied, wondering why he asked me.

"I have heard that he spends his time in teahouses playing the fool." The young man looked very haughty for a moment. I thought, *And you cannot afford such places,* before I replied.

"It is true that he often visits Shimabara. I carry his lantern when he goes."

"It is only a ruse, to fool Kira." The samurai looked sternly at me as if I was thinking of disagreeing with this.

Again stretching my hands out in front of me I bowed my head until it touched the tatami and this time I was allowed to leave.

I couldn't help smiling as I left the rice merchant's house. The voice of the young ronin had had the same quiver of doubt in it as Chikara's had when he repeated, It is only a ruse. Then, recalling the actors, I thought that my master was a good actor as well.

·25·

My Master Eats Sashimi

"Get your lantern ready; we are going tonight. I shall visit not only the teahouse but many other places as well. If anyone asks about me, you know what to say, but try if you can to recall what they looked like. There are two kinds of spies who may be interested in the state of my health and what I am doing: one is Kira's retainers, another is the Shogun's." My master looked at me for a moment. "You are young, Jiro, two years younger than my son." Suddenly he laughed. "I remember when you were born. My wife was very angry at your mother; she wanted her to be shown the gate, told to pass through it and never come back. I was asked to talk to her and find out who your father was." Again Oishi-sama laughed as if he had recalled a joke that pleased him. "She would not tell, even when I threatened her to be beaten with a bamboo cane! Has she ever told you?"

I shook my head and asked, "Was she beaten?"

"No . . . I liked her for it. She had some kind of pride, though I couldn't help wondering who it was. I suspected Matsu for a while, but then thought better of it. He was too shy. If she hasn't told you, she will tell no one, I'm sure."

"I asked more than once, but she never answered, just said something foolish," I mumbled, feeling wretched, for my master's laughter had hurt me. What was so important to me was only a joke to him. I think my master sensed this for he said, "I think it was someone in my house, and that made me feel responsible for you, Jiro. You have been a good and loyal servant and I shall not forget it. Be ready to set out a little before sunset. We shall not return here before sometime tomorrow."

I knew that a meeting was planned for the next day in the temple in Kyoto. I went to the kitchen. My mother was sitting in her usual place eating some leftover rice. Seeing her eating in the middle of the afternoon disgusted me. "My master asked me if I knew who my father was," I said.

"And what did you say?" My mother's hand holding her chopstick was poised halfway between the bowl and her mouth.

"I said I didn't know, and that you wouldn't tell me." I watched the chopsticks, which held a large lump of rice, move to her mouth.

"That's right." The chopsticks descended to pick more rice and I left in a fury. Just as I was about to close the door behind me, my mother called softly, "Jiro! Would you like to know?"

"Yes." I looked back at her.

"It was the Shogun," she said with a malicious grin. I slid the door closed and went to the garden. To my surprise I found that my face was wet with tears.

That night we didn't go to the teahouse that my master usually frequented. Instead, we went to many more lowly places. Here poor samurai and ordinary workers mixed, though the former always seated themselves apart from the others. My master invited many of them to drink with him, and when you're willing to pay, it isn't difficult to find company. I marveled at it, for it was so unlike my master's usual behavior. It was a part he played, but I think he enjoyed it. He had decided to become someone else, a drunken samurai, boastful and coarse. In those low places, there are women as well. They were not high ranking, though some would claim that they once had been such, and in some cases it might even have been true. The sordid gaiety of such places contained sadness as well. Somehow, it struck me — I don't know why — that it was as if not life but death was ever-present here. In most of the places I entered with my master and knelt near him, I got both tea to drink and food. But when one woman handed me sake, Oishi-sama said angrily that I was too young for such. In a way it pleased me, for it showed he cared a little for me.

It was past midnight and I was having a hard time keeping my eyes from closing when a samurai entered and chose to sit near where we were. The place was a little better than some of the others we had visited that night. It served eel, which my master was fond of, and he had ordered a portion for each of us. The samurai called for sake and raw fish, and then turned toward my master and asked if he was not Oishi Kuranosuke. My master smiled and nodded and burped. The samurai frowned. When his sake came he poured some into his cup and then lifting it as if to toast my master, he asked, "And when will you avenge your Lord?"

"Avenge?" My master shook his head and grinned foolishly and then repeated the word. "Avenge . . . Revenge is for fools."

"You mean that you will not avenge your Lord's disgrace?" The samurai's face had grown red with rage. "I thought you a better man than that."

"And I have not thought you better or worse, for I do not know you." My master smiled sweetly and then picked up a piece of eel with his chopsticks and swallowed it as he said, "The food is very good here."

"A samurai who does not avenge an insult given to his Lord is not a samurai." The samurai looked at his raw fish as if it disgusted him.

"In that case there are few samurai in Japan." My master lifted his bowl up near his mouth and stuffed the food into his mouth in a most unseemly manner. Then with his mouth full he repeated, "Revenge is for fools."

The samurai rose and for a moment I feared he was going to draw his sword, and I glanced toward my master's swords, which he had put down on the floor beside him. "Do you like sashimi?" he asked.

"Yes, it goes well with sake. I like especially the tuna." My master pointed to the pieces of raw red fish on the samurai's plate with his chopstick.

"Here, have some." The samurai rose and took a piece of tuna and placed it on his none-too-clean toes. Then he stretched his foot out, inviting my master to eat. Oishi-sama picked it up with his fingers, and popped it into his mouth.

"Delicious," he said and then lifted his sake cup up. Toasting the samurai, he drank. The samurai grabbed the hilt of his sword, then thought better of it, and instead kicked the table where he had sat, turning it over, so fish and sake spilled on the tatami. Then with a toss of his head he strode from the place, while everyone hastily got out of his way.

He was in such a hurry that he forgot to pay. My master shook his head in dismay. Calling the woman who served us over, he said he would pay for the fish since he had partaken of it. The scene had been watched by many, and especially by two samurai who sat so near that they must have been able to overhear everything. Now they asked to pay and left.

I was just about to say something to my master when he said, "Yes, I saw them, Jiro. They will have a story to tell. Now I think you shall light your lamp and we shall make our way to the temple, where we will sleep for the night. I think you are a tired boy."

I nodded and took my lamp to the kitchen, where I had it lit. Then we walked to the temple where we had rooms. I made my master's bedding. The evening was warm and he slid open the doors to the garden. He said he wanted to watch the fireflies for a while. I slept in the corridor outside. As I fell asleep I could hear my master playing his flute.

·26·

I Have a Strange Dream

"Now it is decided. There is no way back." Chikara smiled. We were walking back toward Yamashina; the meeting was over. My master had sent us ahead. He and Otaka Genko would follow later. If there was no way back, then only what lay ahead was of importance. The revenge, the killing of Kira, but beyond that . . .

"What if you can't kill Kira?" I asked. Chikara looked contemptuously at me and said, "Oh my father will find a way."

"Yes." I nodded, for my faith in his father's ability was as great as his own.

"The greatest danger, according to my father, will be if the Shogun suspects our plans. That is why we are to travel to Edo alone or, at most, two together. If too many of us pass through the checkpoints at the same time it is bound to be reported." Chikara grunted and frowned.

"At some of the checkpoints they are more careful than at others," I said, recalling the checkpoint at Hakone, where they had searched not only every bundle we carried, but our clothes as well. On the major roads all over the country the government had established checkpoints that you had to pass through. If you tried to avoid them, because you had no pass or papers, then you could be executed and your head exhibited on a stake.

"When will you be leaving for Edo?" I asked.

"I believe I am to go with Otaka Gengo in a few days. I like Edo much better than Kyoto. Here there are too many merchants who think themselves our masters just because they're rich. The people who serve the Emperor are even worse. They have no respect for a samurai."

"That's true," I said and added, "but they fear you." I had often seen court nobles being carried by in palanquins. They were different from the samurai; their clothes were strangely old-fashioned.

"In Edo everyone fears us." Chikara smiled happily and childishly at the thought.

"I once saw an actor in Edo. He wore a kimono that was very beautiful — maybe it was of silk." I don't know why I said this, and I felt angry with myself for saying it. It was an incident that belonged to me; it meant something to me and I knew it would mean nothing to Chikara.

"Riverside beggars!" Chikara snorted. "If I were the Shogun I would have them all driven out of Edo. I have been told that they dress up as samurai and wear the two swords."

"Maybe they have to. I mean they tell stories by acting them out. Otaka-sama has been to see it."

"Riverside beggars." Chikara repeated the words with obvious pleasure, but as some samurai were passing us just then he said no more.

* * *

"When will you be wearing the two swords?" my mother asked me. "I could lend you two knives from the kitchen."

"Young Oishi-sama wants tea. He says he's hungry as well." I was tired from our long walk, and not in the mood for my mother's jokes.

"There are too many lords around. 'Chikara' still will do for him." My mother nodded emphatically. "He can't grow a beard yet."

Servants complain to themselves and call their masters names, so long as no one can hear them. In that way they rid themselves of their anger and come to some kind of terms with their own miserable condition. Then they can smile again and bow as low as — or even lower than — their master desires. I watched my mother putting a plum inside the rice ball she was making and smiled. Did my mother really think that I had dreams of becoming a samurai? It was impossible, but besides that I had no wish to become one. Did I want to become a rich merchant, as the youngster in the temple had wished and had run away to accomplish? I shook my head. *No, not that either.* Maybe a fisherman. I used to watch them on the beach in Ako. Now, that would be a good life.

"You think too much." My mother had been watching me as she was arranging a tray for Chikara.

"Can one think too much?" I asked, wondering what a strange person I had as a mother.

"Yes. If you think too much, then you can't sleep . . . Bring this in to your young lord." She pushed the tray a tiny bit in my direction. "And when you finally do fall asleep, you have bad dreams."

"That's true." I picked up the tray. "But if one doesn't think there's no point in being alive."

"But there is none anyway," I heard my mother mumble as I left.

Chikara was very much the young lord as I brought him his tray. He expressed his thanks by the tiniest movement of his head. I bowed low and then retired to my little closet of a room. As I lay down to rest I thought about my mother. *She thinks, too, or maybe she really meant it when she said you dream too much. For if you dream too much when you are awake, nightmares may ride you when you fall asleep.*

That night I had a strange dream. I dreamed I was Lord Kira. In my sleep, I, the lowest of servant boys, had suddenly become a Hatamoto, a samurai, a vassal of the Shogun. But though I was such an important person, I was Jiro as well. In dreams one can be anything, even two people at the same time. Lord Kira is an old man, even older than Oishi-sama, but I was not old at all in my dream. I wore very rich clothes, the same I think as I had seen the actor wear. Chikara came to kill me; he had the larger of his swords drawn and came rushing into the room where I was sitting. The room didn't look like a room in a palace but rather like our kitchen. He shouted, "Kira, now you are going to die!" I looked very calmly at him. In my dream I was not the least bit afraid and asked him, "Why do you want to kill me?"

"Because," he shouted, and then he lowered his sword and said in a normal tone of voice, "my father has told me to kill you."

I nodded my head as if I agreed. How strange it is that

in dreams you can see yourself, as if you have suddenly split into two persons, one observing the other.

"But I don't want to die," I declared and pointed to him with my fan. I had no sword.

"But my father says you have to die." Chikara's voice had suddenly become petulant, as it did when we were children and for some reason or another he couldn't get his way.

I shook my head and opened the fan; on it was written the word *Death*. This, for some reason, scared me and I threw it away, and in my dream I could hear it rattle as it fell on the floor. Suddenly a voice said, "Chikara, that is not Lord Kira, that is only Jiro." At this I woke but the voice kept calling, "Jiro." It was my mother — Oishi-sama had come back and I was needed.

"Were you asleep?" my mother asked.

"Yes." I nodded. "I had a strange dream." My mother was standing in the doorway looking in at me; I was still lying down.

"Yes, dreams we are allowed. But maybe it would be best if the Shogun forbade us that." My mother frowned. "Yes, if I was the Shogun I would forbid dreams to anyone who didn't wear the two swords."

"You can't do that, for in dreams anyone can become whatever he desires." As I said this I thought to myself, *I never wanted to become Lord Kira.*

"In dreams" — my mother argued — "the stream is ever upward. Do you think the Shogun's wife ever dreams that she is a kitchen maid? Men, women — all are fools." My mother slid the door closed and was gone, and I, even though I was still tired, got up.

·27·

Otaka Gengo
Leaves for Edo

"I have paid him, Jiro, enough for many lessons yet, so work hard at it; you can't become a rich merchant without being able to write." Otaka Gengo smiled. It was an old joke by now, more like a ritual, and I always consented to becoming a rich merchant.

"I do my best, but some of the letters are very hard to write . . . and to remember." Otaka Gengo had sent someone down to ask me to come to his room in the temple.

"Always sit comfortably when you write, your arms free and loose, and the ink must be neither too thick nor too thin. Also remember, never write when you are angry." The samurai frowned. "That I found difficult to learn. But if your hands are tense in anger you cannot hold the brush as you should, and, besides, what you write down is probably foolish. If you wait until your anger has gone, you will have decided either not to write at all, or to write something that is wise and worthwhile."

"Will you be going to Edo soon, my Lord?" I asked, first agreeing to everything that he had said.

"Tomorrow we shall be leaving. Chikara will be coming with me. You two were friends when you were children?"

"Yes, we played together. I'm younger than he is, by two years."

"Now he is a samurai like his father. He is eager to come, though I think he should have stayed with his mother." Otaka Gengo scowled and I said nothing, for I knew that it was not expected of me to have an opinion on such a matter. "Oh well, the younger children are with her. Still he is young to end his life before it has begun."

"His father asked him if he wanted to take part in the revenge. It was his own choice, or so he told me." I was kneeling in the formal position in front of Otaka Gengo.

"If your father asks you to follow him, even to the land from which no one comes back, you have no choice." Otaka Gengo's features became clouded again. "The word of a father is always a command, even if it is dressed as a question."

"I have none, or at least I do not know who he is, so he cannot command me."

Otaka Gengo smiled. "Maybe you are lucky then, Jiro. You are your own master."

"No!" I protested. "I am everyone's servant." Then, because I didn't want him to think that I minded serving him, I quickly added, "I like serving Oishi-sama; he has been very kind to me."

"Yes." Otaka Gengo nodded. "He is a good master, slow to anger, which means he is seldom unjust. He said he is going to take you with him when he goes to Edo."

I said nothing, just bowed my head low to show that I appreciated the trust that had been shown me. When I looked up again the samurai had taken out a little leather pouch from which he drew a silver ryo.

"Take this, Jiro; I had meant to take you to the theater, since you showed such interest in it. This will be more than enough to gain your entrance."

I took the silver coin from his hand and this time bowed low enough for my forehead to touch the tatami floor. "Thank you," I said twice, then I asked him, "Why are actors called riverside beggars?"

Otaka-sama laughed. "Who told you that?" he asked and I said it was Chikara. Smiling knowingly, the samurai explained it to me. "In the summertime, there is but little water in the rivers. Then the sides of the riverbed make a good place for people to gather. Formerly, the actors, and others as well, took advantage of this to put on shows there. People would come to watch and, when the performance was over, give them a coin or two if they had enjoyed it. But even now, when they have buildings to do their acting in, there are still some who refer to them as riverside beggars."

I nodded to show that I had understood, while I thought with glee, *He doesn't like Chikara that well.*

"Your master will not be leaving for a while. He aims to continue the life he has been living to make Kira and the Shogun believe that he has no thought of revenge. Such behavior is not to his liking; even on the fourteenth of the third month he was seen carrying on as if the anniversary of his Lord's death meant nothing to him. It must be very hard for him."

I told Otaka-sama about the samurai who made my master eat a piece of raw fish from his toes, and his face grew red with anger, but then he laughed.

"You see, Jiro, that I couldn't do. I would make a poor actor. I get angry much too easily. Serve Oishi-sama well, Jiro, for he is worth serving."

That evening we stayed at home. Oishi-sama had asked my mother to buy a fish and other good things for their supper. Otaka Gengo came and much sake was drunk. I saw Chikara with a face the color of the setting sun. We in the kitchen had good food as well; my mother saw to that. The little serving girl was strangely sad. She seldom spoke, but once I noticed that her eyes grew moist, as if she was keeping back tears. She was running back and forth between the main room and the kitchen, serving food and sake. My mother, too, had been near the sake container. I could tell it from the way she behaved. I drank nothing but tea. I'm sure that my mother would have served me sake had I wanted it.

It was late before Otaka Gengo left, past midnight and the moon had set. I saw him to the gate and locked it for the night. When I came back through the kitchen, to check that the fire had been banked, to my surprise I saw that the little serving girl we called Usagi was still awake. She was sitting near the fire, her head in her hands. "What is the matter?" I asked.

"They will leave tomorrow?" she asked.

"I doubt if it will be at sunrise." I laughed. "For that they have drunk too much sake."

"He will never come back." The rabbit lifted her head and now I could see that her cheeks were wet from tears.

"Which one — Chikara or Otaka Gengo — are you crying for?" I asked roughly and a little annoyed.

• 171 •

"Chikara." The girl said this as if the question I had asked was absurd; then she repeated, "He will never come back."

"They are all dead men," I said with disgust. "But what is that to you?"

"He loves me," the girl said and looked down toward the floor or toward her stomach, and I thought, *Is she with child?*

"The only thing they love is their swords and death." I looked at the girl as if I saw her for the first time. She was a very plain little thing, just out of childhood, about the same age as Chikara. "Has he made you with child?" I demanded furiously.

"I love him," she said, with as much defiance as was possible for a rabbit to assume.

"I did not ask that," I said while I thought, *was that the way I was created?* My mother too had been young and plain.

"I don't know," the girl whined. Now tears were running down her cheeks, and in between sobs she repeated her love for my master's son.

"Dry your tears," I commanded. At that moment I hated Oishi Chikara. *We are their slaves,* I thought. *We don't matter, they can do with us whatever they feel like.* The girl dried her face with the sleeve of her kimono. She looked up at me as scared as if she expected me to hit her.

"Go and sleep," I said and smiled, feeling terribly sorry for her. I mumbled, "Maybe he loves you, too, but he has a duty to perform."

"I know," she said and smiled back at me, her eyes still glassy from tears. "He is very brave, and not at all afraid of dying . . . But I am!"

"That is only right. There's nothing wrong in being afraid of it." For a moment I felt like adding, *It's only fools who aren't.*

"He is a real samurai." The girl put such adoration into that word *samurai* that I felt like protesting, and my anger returned.

"Go and sleep, it's late." I touched her hair for a moment and then went to my own room. As I lay down I muttered out loud, *I shall never serve a samurai again* and then made a silent vow to become a fisherman, only to change that promise to a riverside beggar as I fell asleep.

·28·

Chikamatsu Monzaemon Again

As I had been sent with a message, I didn't see Otaka Gengo or Chikara leave. Most of the Ako ronin were leaving or had already left Osaka and Kyoto for Edo. The house felt very empty. I was still taking lessons with the monk in the temple above us. He claimed that I was doing well, but there were still so many more letters to learn. Usagi, the little maid, looked very sad for more than a week; then suddenly I caught her laughing. She was not going to have a child. I felt relieved; I didn't want another miserable Jiro to enter this world. I kept my silver ryo for going to the theater. I had some copper mons as well. But Oishi-sama ventured out on his trips to Shimabara, or any other districts that belonged to the floating world, in the late afternoon, when the theaters were about to close. Their performances would start about an hour before noon and last until almost twilight.

One day, my master had decided to stay at home, because we had come back so early in the morning that I had heard the first cock crow. I asked permission to go, explaining that Otaka Gengo had given me the money for my entrance.

"Yes, the riverside beggars." Oishi-sama looked amused.

"Once when I was your age I saw them in Ako, a troupe of them had come. My father had told me not to go, but I sneaked out and saw them." He laughed as he recalled his own misbehavior. "They are a strange lot; they say that the one whom all the women of Edo love now comes from a family that once wore the two swords."

"I saw him, my lord, when we were last in Edo. He wore clothes of silk."

"Danjuro." My master pronounced the name of the actor with an air of contempt. "Maybe I shall go to see him act when next I am in Edo." Then, looking kindly at me, he said, "Run along, Jiro, and see what lies they are performing this afternoon. Here, whatever your friend Otaka Gengo gave you, I would not like to be thought less generous." From his purse he took out a silver ryo and handed it to me. I bowed and then crawled backward out of the room. Once out on the open road I ran nearly all the way to Kyoto.

The theaters in Kyoto, and in Osaka and Edo as well, were on the outskirts of the city, in the same area as the teahouses. This was by an edict of the Shogun, and no one could open a theater without the permission of the government. You also had to be very careful about what was spoken on the stage, for spies from the Shogunate would often be in the audience and would report it. Should a word be spoken in criticism of those who ruled us the theater would be closed. Because of this the play was often set in days of long, long ago, before the times when a Shogun ruled Japan.

The performance had not yet started when I arrived and paid my entrance fee for the pit. At the side were loges, which had roofs over them and floors of good tatami. The pit, the main part of the theater itself, had only a rough kind of matting covering the stamped earthen floor. Many of the spectators had brought their own mats along to sit on, along with food and sake. I was so eager to get in that I didn't buy any food at the stalls outside the theater. The roof didn't completely enclose the building; on both sides there were open spaces to let in the light, as well as rain when it rained, drenching the audience in the pit. That day was cloudless and very warm. As the theater filled up, the heat and the strong smell of human beings and food was overpowering.

I was fascinated by what I saw. The first play was about Yoshitsune, and dealt with his flight to the north. It may not have been a good play, but to me then it was wonderful. The plight of the young lord, beloved by all, but now homeless, fleeing because of a brother's hatred and envy, moved me to tears. After a pause, when I managed to buy some rice cakes, a comedy was performed. A foolish servant and an equally simple master were traveling to Edo and being taken advantage of by a clever innkeeper. It was indeed very silly, but I laughed over the trickery of the servant, who managed to drink his master's sake. Hardly a word was spoken, but the facial expressions of the actors told the story well enough.

"It is but apery," a voice said near me. I looked around and found myself looking into the eyes of the man called Monza. He smiled and said, "Are you going to tell me how you got your scar?"

"A samurai marked me. He found my face one that was

easily forgotten otherwise." I smiled back and then, refer-
ring to what had just taken place on the stage, I said, "But
this was very funny."

"Oh yes, it is amusing. Always the foolish servant has
got to be just that little bit less foolish than his master. For
the audience loves to see a servant get the better of his
master. Even those in loges." He nodded toward the nearest, where a group of wealthy merchants was seated.
"Though they have servants themselves, when they're in the
theater they will applaud what they would not tolerate in
their own household. Did you like the performance? I don't
mean the apery; it was good enough but I have seen better."

"Oh, yes," I said with a sigh. "It was wonderful."

"It was not." The man looked very severely at me, and
then burst out laughing as he asked me, "How often have
you been to the theater?"

"This is my first visit. But I have wanted to come ever
since I was told about it."

"You know who Yoshitune was. Not only the brother of
the first Shogun, Minamoto Yoritomo, but also a great
general, who in truth had won all the victories that had
made Yoritomo the ruler of the country." I didn't say anything but merely nodded and the man continued, "Now
the Yoshitune you saw strutting around on the stage, can
you believe that he ever led an army, or had ever drawn the
swords from his obi?"

"No," I had to admit. "But he was a fugitive then, I
mean in the play."

"Yes, the loss of power does change a man, but not as
much as that. He acted and looked more like a lost child in

search of his mother than the great general he was." Suddenly he smiled. "I shouldn't spoil your first visit to the theater. Actors and we who write the words they speak are severe critics of the works of others, and I suspect sometimes not hard enough in judging our own. What is your name?"

"Jiro, my lord," I said and bowed.

"My lord. No one has ever called me that, but I like the flavor of it. Some call me master, and maybe some of my work gives me a right to that title. You are a servant of Oishi Kuranosuke?"

"Yes, master," I said and bowed my head.

"And how is Oishi Kuranosuke?" As he asked the question his eyes narrowed and his features grew stony.

Could he be a spy of Kira? I thought. I bowed my head in order not to look into his eyes, and then I mumbled, "I am afraid that my master has taken to drinking too much sake and spends his time in a manner which few people would think right. The teahouse ladies are growing rich as he grows poor." I looked up; now the man was smiling a little.

"How very sad," he said and nodded his head. Then suddenly he laughed once more. "Jiro, it is not only here that plays are acted. There is no place in our country, except for those mountains so high that no man has climbed them, which are not stages, and that includes the Shogun's palace in Edo. The difference between the theater here and the world is that the acting and the lines sprouted by these riverside beggars should be better than what you can hear out in the world, which they weren't today." We were standing, for the performance was over and most of the audience had already departed. "Yes, master," I said, not because I agreed, for I had hardly understood what he meant, but because I felt a response was demanded.

"When that play that you have been given a small part in is over, Jiro, come to me and tell me how it ended."

"The play —" I said, only half understanding what he meant.

"Yes, the first act is well known by now. It took place in the Shogun's palace in Edo and in Ako castle as well. Now the second act, which has been performed here in Kyoto, is I believe almost over, and only the last act is left. Have you played the foolish or the clever servant in what was performed here, Jiro?"

"The foolish servant, master, always the foolish." He was right, it had all been like a play. I had just never thought of it as such.

"One samurai —" I began and then stopped.

"Yes, a samurai, what more?" the playwright asked.

"He said that he believed that actors had no souls and that is why they were actors. He thought they could put on the souls of others as we put on clothes." I had almost made the mistake of telling what Otaka Gengo had said, that one day the revenge they were planning would be acted on the stage.

"He is a clever man, that samurai, and not altogether wrong. They may not have souls, but they have pride and envy enough for a dozen men and that is why I write for puppets now. A puppet has only the soul I give it, and in their wooden heads there is no room for vanity or foolish desires. Have you ever been to the puppet theater?"

"No." I shook my head.

"Come and see one of my plays one day." He put his hand on my shoulder and squeezed it lightly. "A bit of advice: when you speak the truth, you need not speak loudly or look a man in his face; but when you are telling a lie, speak boldly and stare into the face of the man you are talking to, until he looks away. Remember what I asked you. Do come and tell me how it ended." With those words, the man they called Monza turned and walked away. I stared after him and didn't move even when I could no longer see him. Only when a man told me roughly that the play was over and the theater was closing did I become myself again.

·29·

I Find Out Who
My Father Was

I missed Otaka Gengo. I walked up to the temple above our house several times, even though I knew he was now in Edo, but I felt closer to him there. So much did I wish for him to be my father that I asked my mother if she had known him while we lived in Ako. She laughed, grasping what I meant. "Your father was handsomer than that," she said.

"Who was he?" I demanded angrily.

"I told you once already, the Shogun." She spied a tear running down my cheek and relented. "He was a traveling man, I don't even rightly know his name. He had great skill with his tongue." My mother paused and looked out into space, as if she were conjuring up a picture of my father there. "He was a clever man, knew so many words I didn't. Like a silly little fool of a girl, I would have followed him and been his slave. But one morning they were all gone, the lot of them. They had pitched their camp down by the river and that is where they put on their performances. I guess that there were no more loose coppers in the town for them to earn." My mother sniffed and then repeated, "But handsome he was."

A riverside beggar, an actor! I felt so happy that I knelt down in front of my mother and said thank you, as if she had given me a precious gift.

I would have liked to tell someone that I had a father now, even though I didn't know his name or what he looked like. I almost told the young monk who was teaching me to write, but I didn't. But I studied even harder, for now that I knew at least this much about my father — that he knew a lot of words — I too wanted to gain such knowledge. I am afraid that in my mind, I painted a picture of my father that resembled the silk-clad actor I had seen in Edo. It was a great relief that I no longer had to fear that my father was a samurai. Could I have chosen as a parent any man in Japan, including the Shogun, a riverside beggar would have suited me best.

Naturally, this new knowledge made me eager to meet Chikamatsu Monzaemon again. I looked for him everywhere, but he must have gone away. I ate twice in the little soba place where I had first met him, but when I asked the owner of the noodle shop if she had seen him, she shook her head and said that the last time he had been there was when I had been there as well. Had I met him, I would have been sure to tell him about my lately found father. Would he have laughed? I don't know, but I felt almost sure that he would not have. I had decided that as soon as my service with my master was finished, I would become a riverside beggar myself. I felt that this was my right, a right I had inherited from my father. It was not much of an inheritance, but it satisfied me. My life now had a purpose, a goal. I didn't tell my new ambition to my mother; she would just have laughed at me, and later used what she had learned to make further fun of me. As for the rabbit, the little girl we had nicknamed Usagi, she had been present when my mother told me and so heard it all. It made some kind of impression on her, for she would sometimes sigh and look at me with almost the same expression on her face as she had had when looking at Chikara.

My master kept up his excursions into the pleasure quarters all through the summer. I got to know the floating world so well that by the time the oppressive heat was over and the nights had turned cool enough for sleeping, I felt almost as if I had been born into it. If the women in the houses of the floating world are its flowers, then I knew best the roots of such plants — the kitchens, the low taverns, the narrow alleys, where the stink from the river seemed doubly strong. I knew, by sight at least, a lot of rogues. They were arrogantly at ease in the floating world; they belonged there like the rats of the river. Among the servants of the houses I had acquired many friends. I seldom paid for food, for it was freely given to me. This was partly because my master was a good customer and very liberal with his money, but only partly, for I had ingratiated myself with many of the kitchen help by doing small chores for them. To what extent did Oishi-sama truly enjoy himself, and to what extent was it all acting? I shall never know for sure. He was very fond of one woman from that first teahouse he had visited, of that I am sure. She was beautiful, had a lovely voice, and she could play both the samisen and the koto. I have heard her play when it brought tears to my eyes. Her voice was sweet but sad; melancholy, as if she had suffered a tragedy. But then most such women have, for they have usually been sold by their parents to the houses where they work.

It was late in the ninth month, and the landscape had become more brown than green, when my master, on returning from a visit to Shimabara, said, "Jiro, we shall be leaving here in a fortnight, if not sooner. The crooked road must end, and I shall not be sorry." We were very near our house when he said this, and as we came to the gate he stood still. "No, that is not true. I have enjoyed it, or at least parts of it, and there is one person whom I shall be sorry to leave." He shook his head and then, looking at me said, "Jiro, you can tell lies to the world and go unpunished, but never lie to yourself. Good night, boy."

The next night we went again to the floating world, but not to the teahouse where O'Karu was waiting for him. As we passed the building he stood still for a moment, looking at it and smiling to himself. Then he passed on to the lower, more disreputable parts of Shimabara. In a tavern frequented by those whose stomachs usually were as empty as their pockets, Oishi-sama seated himself in a corner and demanded sake. An older woman served him; her kimono was not clean and her obi was askew. Her face was painted, and she smiled as she put the sake down together with two little plates of pickles. I was kneeling nearby. With a cast of his head Oishi-sama ordered, "Tea for the boy."

When my master had drunk two little pitchers of rice wine, a young man entered the tavern. He wore a broad-brimmed hat that almost hid his features. Unceremoniously, he sat down at my master's table, turning his back toward the room. More sake was ordered, and I saw that my master slid a purse into the young man's hand. "It is time," he whispered. "I shall leave within a fortnight."

"Too long has he lived," the young man muttered, and I knew that he meant Lord Kira. "If we had to wait much longer some of us would have had to become dogs of the merchants, or sold our swords."

My master nodded. "I know. Share what I gave you and come to Edo as soon as you can. But do not pass the checkpoints in a group." My master emptied the sake pitcher into his own and the young samurai's cups, and then he said, "Let us drink to the way of the the bow and the horse, even though few samurai can afford such an animal today, and not many of them can bend a bow or hit a target if they could."

The young samurai lifted his sake cup. Mumbling, "The way of the bow and the horse," he emptied it. Then he stood up, bowed, and fled the room.

"Those, Jiro, were the two skills a true samurai had to excel in, the handling of a bow and a horse." We were standing outside the tavern. "That is enough. Let us return home," my master said with a sigh. I had my little lantern lit and walked ahead, pleased that it was not yet midnight. But we were not going to get home that quickly. When we came near the teahouse of O'Karu, we heard wild screams from inside, and a moment later the fat owner of the establishment came rushing into the street, screaming, "Murder, murder." When she spied my master she fell on her knees and begged him to come to her aid. Some blackguards were ruining her house, she cried, and they surely would end up by killing them all.

I could see from the expression on my master's face that

he was not eager to help. But when he heard a particularly loud scream, he drew his sword and entered. I didn't know what to do, but partly out of curiosity I followed.

Two samurai with drawn swords were on a rampage. Much of the furniture had been smashed, and the floor was covered in chips of broken cups, plates, and sake pitchers. The women were all in a corner of the room, screaming at the two men to stop. Somehow this only enraged them more, and had my master not come, it might very well have ended with murder. At the appearance of my master and his command for them to cease destroying the place, they stopped and turned on him. My master asked most politely if they had been cheated or robbed and if that was the cause of their anger. They screamed, "Old man, get out of here before we cut you."

"This is no way for samurai to act." My master answered their insults in a calm voice, which only made them more angry. Both had obviously drank more sake than they could carry. Their faces were red and their legs unsteady.

One of them took a step toward my master and bowed mockingly. "So Oishi-sama is to give us a lesson in behavior, he who spends his time filling his fat belly with sake in the company of whores." At the sound of that word, one of the women stepped forward and, calling the two samurai by names most insulting, shook her fist at them.

The samurai who so far had been silent suddenly lunged toward the woman as if he were going to kill her. She screamed and retreated among the others. The man stopped his pursuit, but, grinning evilly, he said as he scrutinized their faces, "I shall mark you all."

Now I recognized him. It was the samurai who had been the first to spy on us. I looked toward my master; this was bad, for the samurai was, I felt sure, one of Kira's retainers. Now he would have a tale to tell his lord. It was as if my master had understood the danger at the same moment, for very humbly he said, "One must not lose one's temper, even in just anger. Please calm yourself."

"We are not ronin, but retainers of Lord Uesugi. Defend yourself or let me put an end to your feasting and drinking." The first of the samurai whirled his sword about him but did not attack. Lord Uesugi was the son of Lord Kira; he had been adopted by the Uesugi family because it had no male heir.

"Please calm yourself," my master repeated. "You are right. I am but a poor ronin, masterless because of Lord Asano's foolishness. I am an old man and my arm is weak; there would be little glory in cutting me down. Come, let us go and drink some sake instead."

The samurai who had promised to mark the women started to laugh and soon his friend joined him. Their anger gone, they looked at each other; then the samurai who a moment ago had threatened Oishi-sama said, "Why not? Let us lighten his purse and still our thirst at the same time. Oishi lead the way!"

My master grinned as if he was pleased and took them to a nearby tavern. More sake was drunk, until the retainers of Lord Uesugi fell asleep and sank to the floor. I had watched it all from behind a screen that stood near the door. My master rose and paid his bill, giving the owner some more money and telling him not to disturb his two companions but allow them to sleep until they were sober enough to walk home. The owner declared he would, casting at the same time an uneasy glance at his two guests.

"Humiliation is hard to bear, Jiro. I shall have more patience with those old men who are made fun of by the young. How the blood must boil in their veins when they are made sport of by fools. Yet once one's arm grows weak, the sword might as well become rusty." We were standing just outside the tavern. The moon had long set and it would be light in the east before we were home.

"Your arm, my Lord, is still strong," I said.

"It would have pleased me to send them both to a sleep from which they would never waken." Oishi-sama sighed and turned homeward, and I ran to get ahead of him with my little lantern, as was right and proper.

·30·

We Return to Edo

Strangely enough, the loss of face, the humiliation he had experienced in the house of O'Karu, seemed to have depressed my master far more than when he had been forced to eat raw fish from the foot of the samurai. Was that because O'Karu had witnessed his shame? She had been among the women, and I thought it might even have been she who had shouted at the two samurai. The following day my master stayed in his room, and when I served him his meals he spoke not a word to me, only nodded or made a motion with his hand to show that he was aware of my existence. The following day he went to the temple and though he spent a long time in prayer, he was silent and glum when he returned. A week went by without Oishi-sama stirring from the house or garden, and I began to wonder if he was not well. But he did not look sick, and he would exercise in the garden with his sword, one moment averting an attack, the next lunging at an imaginary enemy.

On the sixth day of the tenth month, he told me to be ready the next day for traveling to Edo. That day he left the house, ordering me to pack clothes. I think he went to Kyoto. Was he going to see O'Karu for a last time? When he returned a little before sunset, he had a giant of a man with him. I recognized him right away. He was called Uma; what his real name was I do not know and I doubt if he did. In Ako he had worked in the stables, and it was because of his work that he had been nicknamed Uma, horse. He was strong as a bear, but very gentle; he loved the horses that he looked after, and only mistreatment of the beasts in his care could make him angry. He was a very simple man, more like a giant ten-year-old child than a man who had passed his thirtieth year.

"Do you remember me, Jiro?" he asked. My master had ordered me to take him to the kitchen and see to it that he was fed.

"You are big enough to be noticed and difficult to forget once seen," I answered with a grin. "Are you hungry?"

"I have had nothing to eat today and not much more yesterday. My stomach keeps shouting at me, 'I am hungry,' and I keep telling it to be patient."

My mother was pleased to see Uma, and as she had just cooked the rice for our supper, she gave him a bowlful. She asked him a lot of questions about Ako, and the giant answered as best as he could with a mouth full of rice. It did not take him long to empty his dish, and he looked so longingly at the pot of rice that my mother laughingly dished out another bowlful. He thanked her so earnestly that I could not help laughing and I asked him if his stomach was still shouting.

"Jiro, that belly of mine is like a bottomless hole. I think it could hold a koku of rice and still have space left over for a fish." Uma looked pleadingly at my mother, but she acted as if she hadn't heard him.

"You were lucky to meet Oishi-sama," I said. Uma nodded and smiled; then he lifted one finger and shook it at me. "It was not altogether just luck. Yesterday I went to the shrine of O'Inari and prayed to those little foxes most earnestly, and my stomach was grumbling so loudly that I am sure O'Inari heard it and took pity on me."

"You mean the foxes led you to Oishi-sama?"

"I sat all day in front of the shrine, the one near the temple with the gate that was built by our Lord Asano. And just at the moment when I was about to give up, there came Oishi-sama, and when he saw me, he said, 'Uma, how are your legs and your feet? Are they strong enough to carry you to Edo?' I said, 'If only my stomach is filled I could walk as far, and carry two kokus of rice as well.' 'That is good, Uma,' he said, 'for I have only a boy to attend me, and I need someone to carry our baggage. We shall fill that stomach of yours, and you shan't have to walk any farther than Edo. And here I am." Uma grinned and held out both his hands.

"That's good, because I was beginning to worry that I couldn't carry all that our master wants to take with him." This was true. The bundle was huge, and I had already given up taking anything of my own along.

"Don't worry, I shall carry it, and if you get tired you can sit on my shoulders as well. If only I get rice enough, then my legs and arms get strong, but without food I feel very weak, like a newborn child." Uma looked at the pot of rice and then at my mother beseechingly.

I laughed, imagining Uma as a newborn child, but somehow I couldn't believe he had ever been small. My mother looked into the rice pot, wrinkled her brow, and said, "You can have half of Jiro's portion." And with those words she filled up the giant's bowl once more.

"Thank you." Uma bowed toward me and then gobbled up the food. I laughed for I wasn't that hungry, and I was pleased to have a companion for the journey to Edo, especially one as strong as Uma.

We left for Edo early in the morning. Uma did carry the large bundle containing my master's clothes, writing material, brushes and inkstone, plus some papers. I carried only my own little bag. The morning was cool and it was pleasant to walk, but by midday it was very warm. We rested in the shade of a large pine tree that grew in front of a little tavern. Our master bought us food but ate little himself.

There is not much to tell of such a trek: you walk until you are so tired that at night you sleep the moment you lie down. There were other travelers on the road; once a great lord passed with his retinue. My master knelt as the daimyo passed; we more ordinary men who were not allowed to carry weapons lay outstretched upon the ground.

At Hakone, near the lake in the mountains, is an important checkpoint that we had to pass through. The primary reasons for these checkpoints were that no powerful daimyo should be able to move his soldiers about without the Shogun's knowledge, nor could his wife or children leave Edo, where they were kept as hostages. Once, nearly a hundred years ago, the great lords of Japan had fought each other for power and laid waste the country. Shogun Tokugawa Tsunayoshi was not going to allow that to happen again.

When we came near the checkpoint, my master stood still for a moment. He looked down upon the ground, then at Uma, and finally at me. "My name is —" He paused and then said a name I had never heard before. "We come from Osaka and you have not been long in my service." I gasped, for this was dangerous. To give a false name at a checkpoint was no better than trying to evade it by climbing the mountains. I nodded to show that I had understood. "As for you" — Oishi-sama turned to Uma — "you can't remember my name. I have hired you just for the trip. You are a fool so act as if you don't understand anything." Poor Uma nodded as well, but he looked very confused, and a little unhappy at being called a fool. When Oishi-sama walked on I whispered to him, "He wants you to act as if you were not very clever. So if they ask you something, just grin and shake your head." Now Uma understood and he smiled happily: he wasn't a fool; he only had to act like one.

My master handed his papers to the samurai, who looked us over carefully. He paid the least attention to Uma; it was probably beneath his dignity to notice such a beast of burden. He read the name on the paper out loud and looked long at my master. Oishi-sama stared back at him as if he had not a care in the world. The samurai smiled thinly, then indicated to his assistant that we could pass through. But before he let us go he said in a low voice, almost a whisper, "You look like someone I once knew. If you were he I would wish you good luck."

My master bowed, acknowledging what was said, and then with a motion of his hand bade us to follow him. The checkpoint is a long house with many rooms; the guards were not samurai, and one I saw carried a strange long-handled fork with two prongs. When we could no longer see the building I drew a sigh of relief. I wondered if the samurai had recognized my master and wished him luck. Near the checkpoint building I had seen a field of execution, where a couple of heads had been exhibited. If some other samurai had been on duty, who did not feel sympathy for our cause, then our heads might soon have been there for the crows to eat. Uma grinned. He hadn't been aware that he had been in any danger.

To my surprise, we didn't go directly to the inn where we had stayed last time in Edo. Instead, we stopped in Kamakura. We stayed not at an inn but at a temple. The priest seemed to know my master, and they held long conversations late into the night. Uma and I explored the city, and we saw the giant statue of Buddha. Kamakura is a beautiful city and contains almost as many temples as Kyoto.

On our second day there, two of Lord Asano's retainers came, and my master spent the whole day with them. They left after dark, the monks in the temple having made their food. They drank a good deal of sake as well, and their faces were red when they left. It was a full moon and I couldn't sleep, partly because I shared a room in one of the sheds with Uma. He had no trouble sleeping and snored like a dragon. The garden was not large but very lovely; there was a pond with stepping stones to cross it. I sat at its shore under a willow tree, thinking about what was going to happen. The two ronin had been so happy, so excited; had it never occurred to them that they were about to give up

their lives? Suddenly, out from the sha
stepped a figure, a man. In the moonlight
it was my master; he went to the pond
staring into the water as if he saw something
worth contemplating. I sat perfectly still, n
move. Suddenly he sighed deeply and then
walked back toward the temple.

I felt sorry for him, a feeling that I had never ha
As I went back to my own sleeping place I stood
pond where he had stood, and as I looked down I saw
of a water lily that was just about to burst into bloom.
that what he had been looking at, or had he not seen it?

On the fourth day, we left Kamakura for a cottage in t
country near Kawasaki. We stayed ten days there, and al
most every day someone would come from Edo to report
how things were there. A couple who did the cooking there
had been Lord Asano's servants in his mansion in Edo,
where his wife had been forced to live, as a hostage of the
Shogun when Lord Asano was in Ako. They seemed very
attached to the family and treated my master as if he were
their Lord. I had little to do, though I did sometimes serve
sake to the Asano ronin who came. From what I heard,
nearly all the samurai who had signed with their blood to
avenge their master were now in the city, waiting.

I was eager for us to move to Edo, because that would
mean that I would see Otaka Gengo again, and though I no
longer wished that he was my father, I was very fond of
him. On the first day of the eleventh month we left and by
evening of that day we were again lodged in the little inn
near Nihombashi.

Otaka Gengo
Masquerading as
a Rich Merchant

I was disappointed that Otaka Gengo was not there. I had expected him to be waiting for us. Instead, several of the Asano ronin were there, none of whom noticed me. I had gotten used to Uma, the kind giant, but he was sent away to stay somewhere else. My master laughingly declared that he was too conspicuous to keep around. I think he was fond of Uma, but in the same way he would have been fond of a favorite horse.

Little was asked of me, so I drifted around the streets, all the while hoping to see the silk-clad actor once more. The second day I was there I saw a wealthy merchant carried by in a palanquin. As he passed he spotted me and ordered his bearers to halt. Then, in a petulant voice he called, "Boy, come here!" I obeyed, bowing as I got nearer the litter. Standing with my head humbly bent, I stared at my feet.

"Ragamuffin! Look at me!" the merchant ordered. I did, and my eyes opened wide in surprise. It was Otaka Gengo. "Child of the sewer, I have use of you. Meet me at the hour of the monkey, in that small sake shop down there." Otaka-

sama pointed down a little alley. "Here, guttersnipe, hold out your hand." I obeyed and two copper coins were dropped into it. "Beasts of burdens, carry on!" At this command the litter carriers moved on at a stately pace.

Some of the merchants were so ill-bred that they would use such language as Otaka Gengo had, but a samurai cared too much for his dignity to stoop that low. No, that is not true, some would, but not my master or most of the Ako ronin. Obviously Otaka Gengo was enjoying himself masquerading as a rich merchant. I put the coins he had given me into my sleeve. "The hour of the monkey," I whispered to myself. "I wish it was now." But it wasn't; the hour of the monkey is in the late afternoon and now it was just a little past the middle of the day.

Long before the time appointed I was back, exploring the alley. It was not a place where you would meet a rich man, and the sake shop looked as shabby as one would expect its customers to be. At the very moment when I judged the hour of the monkey had begun I entered the place. It was empty. It was probably a little too early for its regular clients. I seated myself in a corner and ordered tea, declaring that I was waiting for someone. The woman was coarse and fat, heavily made up in the fashion I was used to from the floating world. These women always remind me of spiders, the teahouses and taverns being the nets they have woven.

"Is it your master you are waiting for?" she asked me as she brought the tea. I nodded and was about to pour the tea when she told me to wait a little and asked if I would not care for a cake. At the mention of the word, I suddenly felt hungry and said I would. She brought a little plate with two bean-paste cakes on it, and then knelt down as she poured my tea. "Are you from here?" she asked.

The women who run these little sake or noodle shops are always terribly nosy, but since I saw no reason for not telling her, I said I came from Ako.

"I come from Kyoto. Edo may be the eastern capital but Kyoto is the western and the true one. As east and west are opposites, so are the towns. True elegance you will not find here; the women are coarse and the men brutes." The woman shook her head in dismay.

"If you do not like Edo, why do you live here?" I asked, wondering if she had ever been elegant or beautiful.

"My parents were very poor so they sold me. I was in the Yoshiwara for ten years, and earned money enough to buy this."

"The floating world," I said; it was strange that so few of the girls sold into that world where night becomes day seemed to resent it.

"You are too young for that yet." The woman laughed. "But I was considered very beautiful then. I lived in the floating world ten years but I didn't drown." She looked with pride around her little sake shop. "I hope your master will come soon and that he will drink something stronger than tea."

I nodded and picked up one of the cakes she had served me and bit into it. It was surprisingly good, wrapped in a leaf with a little red plum on top for decoration. I thought of my mother, and decided that I would buy her some of the best cakes that could be bought in Kyoto as soon as I was back. I stretched out my legs, sipped my tea, and ate the second cake. Half the hour of the monkey had gone before Otaka Gengo arrived, and I had drunk several pots of tea and eaten two more cakes.

"Jiro, I shall leave you my merchant disguise." Otaka Gengo sat down across from me. Looking at my teapot and cup, he laughed. "I am an expert now; there is nothing I don't know about the ceremony of tea drinking. I doubt if even the greatest of tea ceremony masters could find me at fault. Did you realize that not only the quality of the tea is of great importance? Even more precious is the value of the utensil you drink it out of."

"What do you desire, master?" The lady of the house was kneeling in front of the ronin.

"Some sake," Otaka Gengo ordered. "And I do not care, my late autumn flower, about the quality of the vessel you bring it in, but as for the sake I prefer it not diluted with water from the river."

"I serve only the best of sake, master." The woman bent her head twice and then rose to fulfill the order.

"Your legs were not worn shorter by the long trip from Kyoto." Otaka Gengo smiled and looked me over to see that I had not grown shorter.

I told him about the guards at Hakone checkpoint, and that my master had given a different name. I also told him that Uma had come along to carry our baggage and this made Otaka Gengo laugh.

"I tell you, Jiro, there is no woman in all of Japan who takes as good care of her husband as Uma did of the horses in his charge. When one of the mares was sick I found him crooning a lullaby to it."

The woman had brought the sake and some little bowls of herbs and tiny squids. She had given me a cup as well and my friend filled it. "Drink it, Jiro; it warms your belly."

My friend; this is the first time I have written that. But Otaka Gengo was my friend, even though the distance between us was as great as between Kyoto and Edo. Just because I was so happy to see him again, I burst out telling him about my mother finally admitting who my father was.

"A riverside beggar." Otaka Gengo laughed. "I have often wondered who in the household was your father. Oishi is fond of you. I even thought he might have sired you. A riverside beggar." Again the samurai laughed. But then seeing that I looked hurt he quickly said, "They are a clever lot, some of them, if not all of them, for in that world a fool doesn't survive long. Will you try to find him and claim your inheritance?"

"My mother does not remember his name; she only said he was handsome." I smiled and emptied my cup, feeling suddenly foolish. Otaka Gengo sensed it and, filling my cup once more, he said, "Do you want to be an actor yourself?"

"Yes, I would like to," I answered in a low voice, looking away. "But I don't know how."

"You will find a way, if you really want to. I don't know what it is like; you must learn to creep inside another man's soul if you are to succeed." Suddenly Otaka Gengo laughed again. "You may someday creep into mine, and strut like me on a stage." Seeing the incredulous look on my face he added, "Oh, they will make a play out of us, that you can be sure of. But if you're going to play me, then try to understand me. Do not make fools out of us."

"But why are you going to do it? The Lord of Ako is dead, it can make no difference to him." I looked at the samurai; truly he was my friend or I would not have dared to say what I had just said.

"You are not . . ." Otaka Gengo began and then, seeing the expression on my face, stopped and leaned across the table and touched my hand. "I am sorry, Jiro, our Lord had more than two hundred retainers and we are not more than a fourth of that number willing to revenge Kira's insult to the Lord Asano. Maybe they, too, were not truly samurai." Otaka Gengo poured himself another cup of sake, and drank a sip of it. "You have an idea of what you are. It is as if you can see yourself, your image. You do not want this picture of yourself tarnished. Death is the end of you, but the image remains, as pure as when you were alive. If I had sold myself to anyone who would have cared to buy me, then I would be alive, but my soul would be dead. I am fond of life, don't for a moment think I'm not." The samurai drank the last of the sake and then sighed. "But I would rather be dead and the image of myself alive than the other way around." He emptied the last few drops of sake from the pitcher into his cup and ate the last of the pieces of squid. "Do you understand it, Jiro? If you want to be an actor you must learn to."

"I do," I said, feeling both sad and strangely happy at the same time.

"Some of Lord Asano's retainers, I among them, had parents or even grandparents who had served him. We had been well paid and kindly treated. What happened to him was an injustice, and any injustice changes the world. The sky, the stars, even the lantern of night, grow dim in shame. When we kill Kira, we shall put it right once more."

I nodded, for I did understand what he meant. But there is so much injustice and yet the stars are bright and the moon rises in the night, wanes and grows full again. But I suppose not to him or to my master Oishi-sama.

"It will happen very soon." Otaka Gengo rose, and I noticed that he was wearing a very plain kimono. The hilt of a sword protruded from his obi; I couldn't help glancing at it.

The samurai's hand touched the hilt. "Soon I can throw it away and wear my own; the blade of my sword is not rusty, but clean and shiny as moonlight on the water. When it's done, go back to Kyoto, Jiro, and learn the art of putting on other men's souls the way you take on their clothing." Otaka Gengo threw some coins on the table and left.

The proprietor, who had been watching, rushed over quickly and scooped up the money. She was afraid that I would take some of it. I grinned. If there was no elegance in Edo, she was in the right place. She bowed deeply as I left. Otaka Gengo had overpaid.

·32·

The Day of Revenge Is Near

The innkeeper where we were staying was trustworthy. Lord Asano's samurai when they were in Edo had used the inn often. But even then most of our visitors would come late in the evening when the streets were dark. My master had meetings with the younger samurai as well, but these were always held in faraway places. Secrecy was of the greatest importance, for if the Shogun got word of the planned revenge, all the retainers of Lord Asano would be rounded up immediately and sent into exile. Those who were exiled to distant lonely places seldom returned.

I was often sent on errands, for who notices a boy, unless he wants to be noticed? The samurai had been divided into four groups, each with a leader. Most of them did not wear their swords, but were disguised as ordinary citizens of the town; they were often dressed as workmen, tradesmen, or even servants. I couldn't help laughing to myself at some of them, for they would strut in their servants' dress as arrogantly as when they had swords stuck in their obis. Sometimes I would see Otaka Gengo being carried by in the street, the rich merchant. He had become friends with a tea ceremony teacher who was friendly with Lord Kira, and he had even been invited into the house of the enemy. I didn't see him very often, but when I did he always had a smile for me, and a few words to show that he had not forgotten me.

The last month of the year came and the weather turned very wintry. The wind came from the east bringing snow, and I was very cold. When sent on an errand I hurried, and my poor feet were cold and blue. When I came back the cook would give me warm water to wash them in, but soon they would be cold again. The houses in Edo, as in Kyoto, were built for summer heat rather than winter winds.

Our inn was not far from Nihombashi bridge. Once I was sent with a message to a samurai who lived across the river. I had just reached the center of the bridge when a voice commanded me to halt. Two samurai were about a hundred yards behind me. I recognized one of them, the one who had marked me with his sword. I ran, but I had not gone far before a hand caught me and slung me to the ground. I could hear the samurai who had ordered me to halt coming from behind and shouting "thief" he ran to catch me. The man who had stopped me was a samurai whom I had never seen before. He put his foot on my chest as I sprawled on my back. I looked up at him. "These men are enemies of my master," I stammered.

"It is well that you caught him; he belongs to a band of thieves," the samurai declared, out of breath and grinning as he looked at me. My captor took his foot off my chest and with a motion of his hand told me to get up. "What has he stolen?" he demanded.

"I marked him last time he tried to take my purse. That was in Kyoto; he seems to have taken his trade to Edo now."

"I have never stolen anything," I declared, appealing to the stranger who had his hand on my shoulder. "My master takes good care of me; I have no need to steal."

"His master is a ronin," the samurai who had once scarred my forehead declared. "He is no better than a highwayman. Let me take him with me."

"And whom do you serve?" my captor asked, letting go of my shoulder, and scrutinizing my enemy with a none-too-friendly eye.

"I am a retainer of Lord Uesugi," he stammered, ill at ease.

"He keeps his men poorly dressed. Has he lost his domain?" My captor smiled; his own dress was splendidly rich. "And you, whom are you a retainer of?" he demanded of the second samurai, who had just caught up with his friend.

"I serve Kira Kozukenosuke," he declared and bowed.

"I think you both serve Kira Kozukenosuke, and he is known for liking gold too much to part with it." The hilts of my captor's swords were inlaid with gold.

"That is true enough." The samurai grinned cheerfully. "Our lord does not give a silver coin away without getting a gold one in return."

"There you are." A man dressed in workman's clothes bowed deeply to my captor. "I hope, my lord, he has not caused you trouble. He is my apprentice, I am a carpenter, and his father has paid me to make a craftsman of him." I immediately recognized the "carpenter"; it was Okajima-sama in disguise. I looked down at my feet, crestfallen.

The Kira retainer who had marked me once with his sword now pointed a finger at Okajima-sama and, raising his voice almost to a shout, he said, "That fellow is no carpenter, he is a ronin, one of the retainers of that fool Asano. No one will employ them as they are known as a dishonest crowd." Quickly I glanced around, taking in the scene. Okajima-sama's face was purple with rage.

"I was in Ako once." My captor's voice was low as he recalled his visit to the town. "Lord Asano treated me well; I stayed in his castle a week. I regret what happened to him, as do most people and all who knew him." The samurai's hand went to the hilt of his sword as he fondled it. Raising his voice a little and turning to the two Kira samurai, he said, "I think you have made a mistake. It must have been some other boy who tried to steal your purse." Then turning to me he observed, "They all look alike. Take him with you, my good man, and go in peace."

I felt Okajima-sama's hand grab my neck and, mumbling thank yous, we hurried away. The two Kira retainers were silent. Glancing back, I saw them bow deeply to my captor. I wondered who he was, a high-ranking retainer of some lord.

"You should not be running around here in the streets, Jiro. Those were Kira samurai; now they will know that your master is in town. They will warn Kira and all might be lost." Okajima-sama was still holding on to my neck, and I almost feared he would break it, for he was very strong. "What were you doing, anyway?" he demanded.

"I was sent on an errand," I squeaked. At this he let go of my neck. "Oishi-sama sent me," I added in a normal voice.

"Well, you'd better go then and do it, whatever it was,"

Okajima-sama grumbled. "But maybe you should wait until those Kira rascals are gone." We had stopped not far from the inn and the samurai put his hand on my shoulder to show that he was not angry anymore.

"I don't have to," I said. "Oishi-sama had sent me to you, to tell you to come, for he had some news for you."

Okajima-sama laughed. "So that was the errand. Too bad that I spent too long getting dressed or I would have been here before you left, and this would not have happened. He was the one who marked you? Well, I shall mark him, I promise you that, Jiro."

Since Okajima-sama had always been friendly to me I dared ask, "Who was the lord who caught me, the one with the golden sword hilt?"

"I think he is a retainer of Date Sakyonosuke, Lord of Yoshida. He knew who I was. Some say that Lord Date should have prevented our Lord from wounding Kira. Most if not all of his retainers are on our side. But come with me, for you'd better tell your master what happened. I came late so I did not see or hear it all."

My master was not too upset by the incident. A few days later, at a meeting of the older and more important of Lord Asano's retainers, the day for the revenge was decided. I was naturally not told, but a look at the solemn faces of the Asano ronin there made me sure that it was to be soon. Otaka Gengo was in attendance. As he left he nodded his head toward me, but he did not smile as he usually did. Chikara had been staying in the inn with his father; most of the time he felt too far above me to talk to me. But every once in a while he forgot himself, I think out of loneliness, for he was too young to have any near friendship with the other Asano ronin.

"Jiro," he said the very next day, "Jiro, it will be soon." I nodded and smiled as if I too rejoiced at this news, and maybe I did. "No date could be better," he added, and demanded that I bring him some tea.

No date could be better, I repeated to myself as I went to fetch it. Now I knew the appointed time. It would indeed be soon, in five days' time, on the fourteenth, for had not Lord Asano been ordered to commit seppuku on the fourteenth?

·33·

The Night Before

On the eleventh of the month it started to snow; all night
it continued, and by morning the city wore a cloak of white.
The day was cloudy and cold, and the sun was hidden all
day so the snow did not melt. It was very beautiful, and the
town turned oh so quiet. People stopped each other in the
street, to comment upon the great snowfall. "Never has
there fallen so much snow," was the remark on everyone's
tongue. On the evening of the twelfth the clouds grew
darker and the snow began to fall again, and this time it
continued the following day as well. Otaka Gengo declared
that it was the cherry trees of the gods that were losing their
flowers. That night for a short while the moon emerged
between the clouds. I was not asleep, though the whole
town was, and walked to Nihombashi bridge. The water
was silver in the moonlight, and all the roofs of the houses
along the river glittered as if tiny stars were buried in the
snow. I stood there until the clouds again swallowed the
moon and my feet were so cold that I feared they would fall
off. Just as I turned to go back to the inn a voice near me
said, "Yes, just a night for poets and riverside beggars to
be out in." Surprised, I looked in the direction from which

the voice had come. It was Otaka Gengo; he, too, had found himself too restless to sleep.

"It was lovely when the moon came out," I said, and just at that moment, for only the shortest of time, it peeped out again and illuminated the samurai's face.

"Soon I shall have to say goodbye to you, Jiro. I wish you luck." Then he drew his sword a little way out of its scabbard. It was not made of wood; the moonlight lit its steel.

"Tomorrow," I whispered, as the moon again disappeared beyond a bank of dark snow-filled clouds.

"Today, for it is now the hour of the ox, and past the middle of the night. Go home, Jiro, and sleep . . . Soon I shall sleep the sleep that no one wakes from. I must go to my room and write a letter to my mother, who is still alive, to tell her why I must throw away the gift she gave when she bore me. For a moment I envy you, you little riverside beggar who shall live to watch the moon's dance across the sky and feel the soft breezes blow when spring comes to our land." Otaka Gengo sighed and then laughed softly. "But I tell you, Jiro, by dying we shall live forever." The darkness swallowed up my samurai friend, and the soft snow the sound of his footsteps.

As I lay down to sleep I thought, *He does not want to die.* I found comfort in that. I did not want him to cast away his life, as if that gift were not precious, but something of so little value that it could be thrown away without regret. It took me long to fall asleep, and when I did, I had a strange dream, of a dark turbulent river that I had to cross, knowing that it was so deep that I would surely drown. Just as the water engulfed me, I woke up. One of the servants in the inn was touching me with his big toe, telling me to rise, that it was morning and my master was calling for me.

Still sleepy-eyed, I went to Oishi-sama's room and knelt in front of him. He was eating his breakfast, and for a while he did not speak, but contemplated me. I bent my head so that I did not look at him.

"Jiro," he finally said, "the house in Yamashina I have given to the temple; they have promised to keep your mother there, and to make a priest out of you if you wish it. If you do, you might pray for us." My master ceased and looked at me.

"Even if I should not devote my life to Buddha, I shall never forget what I owe you, and no day shall go by in which I do not remember you, and I shall say no prayer in which your name is not mentioned." I was moved because Oishi-sama had thought of my mother and me. I felt my eyes grow wet, and therefore I looked down again at the straw-matted floor.

"I want you to leave here tomorrow morning, for when I depart tonight I shall never return. The Shogun might send men to arrest you on some charge or another, because you are my servant. His men would not harm a dog, but would torture a boy if they thought he knew something of value to them. Here is a pass that will get you through the checkpoints, and here is a purse that contains enough so that you won't starve on your journey. But be careful and have it well hidden, sleep in the stables of the inn, and do not let anyone know that you could pay for better."

I took the pass, a piece of paper that bore the seal of a

great lord, and the purse, which Oishi-sama had placed on the table in front of him. Then I bowed twice so deeply that my forehead touched the floor.

"I have been well satisfied with you, and if you do not wish to serve Buddha, then remember the seal on the pass. If you tell that lord you have served me, then I think room could be found for you among his servants."

Again I bowed, but while I did, I thought, *No, I will never serve a samurai again. I will be a riverside beggar, and if I cannot be that, then I will go to some little village by the sea and learn to fish.*

"Now, Jiro, go and tell them to bring me some fresh tea; the water was not hot enough. And then leave me undisturbed, for I have some letters to write. If anyone comes, tell them to wait and see that they are served tea."

I crawled slowly backward out of the room. As I slid the door closed, I glanced at my master. His brow was furrowed; though he was looking at me I felt sure he no longer saw me.

It was not long before our first visitors came. They were the older and more important samurai of the Asano clan. The only younger person there was my master's son Chikara, whom the others treated very respectfully in spite of his youth. I think this was because they felt sorry for him, for he was so young to lose his life. Chikara was not aware of this, and he was obviously enjoying his own importance.

"Jiro." Otaka Gengo was one of the last to come. I met him in the entrance hall of the inn. "I see they are all here." He was looking at the footwear on the floor. I nodded and said that my master was writing letters but he would soon be free. "I wrote mine; it was hard to write, and the longer the letter became, the less satisfied I was with it. But it will have to do; there is no more time for brush and ink." The samurai removed his straw sandals; they were of double thickness. I took his sandals and turned them on the earthen floor of the hall so they faced the entrance. Otaka Gengo was watching me, a smile on his face. "I have little to leave anyone, my silver is almost used up. But here, Jiro, is a little purse. I value it, for my mother made it; in it you will find two silver coins and a few copper mons. You will need them for your trip back to Kyoto."

"My master," I said, "Oishi-sama, has already given me money." Very confused and unhappy, I bowed to him.

"He is fond of you." Otaka Gengo looked kindly at me. "But if you don't want to serve a rich merchant — and that is still my advice — it will save you from having to do any begging from your riverside the moment you are back." The samurai placed the purse in my hands, and I touched it to my forehead as I declared my thanks. As I watched Otaka Gengo disappear, joining the others I thought, *Yes I would serve him, and to death too.* Maybe that was the way he felt about Lord Asano, and then maybe the whole thing made sense.

In the afternoon Oishi-sama and the older samurai went to Sengakuji Temple to pray at the grave of Lord Asano. In a room in the temple the final instructions were given. I was still at the inn, but I learned that two groups were to attack the front of Kira's mansion, the other two the rear. The passwords were Yama (mountain) and Kawa (river). Whoever could not answer "Kawa" when someone shouted

"Yama" was to be treated as an enemy. They were ordered not to fight anyone, unless they resisted, for it was only Kira they wanted to kill. If they should fail, they were to commit seppuku after they had set fire to the mansion.

To my great surprise, I learned when my master returned to the inn that the band that was to attack the rear of the mansion was to be led by Chikara. *He is naught but a boy still,* I thought, but then I heard that two of the older samurai were to be his co-captains, and I understood that it was to honor not Chikara but his father that he had been chosen.

I had been ordered to see to it that water was heated so that my master and his son could bathe. After their bath they ate alone. I served them instead of the usual servant of the inn. They spoke little to each other but ate with hearty appetites, and had a few cups of sake. "Tomorrow it will be over," Oishi-sama said, lifting his cup and looking at his son. "May we succeed."

Yes, I thought kneeling at the door, *tomorrow it will be over, and then I shall return to Kyoto and tell the man they called Monza what I have seen and heard.*

·34·

The Revenge

I helped my master and Chikara to dress; they wore no clothes that had been worn before, as people do when they marry. In a way I suppose they were getting married, wedded to their fate. Then they put on the armor, and my master's was a tight fit, for he had gained weight from his visits to the floating world. They burned incense in their helmets. At last they were ready. Oishi-sama stood for a moment looking around the room, as if he wanted to remember what it looked like. Then he walked out, his son following him. I waited for just a very short while, then I, too, left.

Hara Soemon and Mase Kyudaiyu, two of the oldest of the retainers of Lord Asano, were waiting for my master. They were more splendidly dressed than I had ever seen them before. The innkeeper was in the hall, bowing as if his back had a hinge on it. "We have been well satisfied," my master said and glanced for a moment at the man. Turning to his companions he said, "It is time." They nodded gravely; then, as my master left with Chikara following close, they, too, departed. They did not close the sliding door behind them, and in the light from the lantern hanging outside and proclaiming the name of the establishment, I could see snowflakes falling.

"That is lucky, few will be out in this weather," the innkeeper said as he closed the door.

"Yes," I agreed, and thought, *They did not notice me as they left.*

I must see it all, I thought, while replying to the innkeeper, who had asked me if I was to stay in Edo, that I would be leaving in the morning.

"That will probably be best for you," he agreed. Yawning and stretching himself, he bade me good night. I went to a little cupboard where I had been allowed to keep my few possessions and packed them into a bundle that would be easy to carry. The house was very still. It was past midnight. I knew that the attack on Lord Kira's house was to take place in the beginning of the hour of the tiger. Then there would be only a few hours to the dawn, but it is the time of night when people sleep most soundly and few are awake. I put away my bundle in the closet; I would retrieve it later. Then I let myself out the door of the inn.

No wind was stirring. The snowflakes were falling straight to the earth. I wore but thin straw sandals on my feet and had not gone far before they felt very cold. Kanzaki Yogoro, one of the retainers of Lord Asano, had a small shop and there the weapons were kept. I had been there often with messages, so I knew my way. A lantern was burning outside the shop, illuminating a circle in the snow. I drew close to the walls of the neighboring house and waited. A group of samurai came out from the house. In the light from the lantern I recognized a face or two. Some

were carrying spears, others halberds; all wore helmets and were dressed in armor. Suddenly the street was filled with them, but I couldn't see if my master or Chikara was among them. On a word of command, which I could not understand, they formed a line, three deep, and, led by Kanzaki, they marched in the direction of Lord Kira's mansion. I followed, keeping a distance for fear I would be recognized and told to go back.

Near the mansion they were met by some of the older samurai, among them my master. They led the band now; the younger ronin were carrying bamboo ladders to scale the walls. The street was broad in front of Lord Kira's mansion, forming a little square; it was covered in newly fallen snow, clean and white, like paper not yet touched by the brush.

So far all had been silent. They split into two groups; one, among them the younger ronin led by Chikara, went to the rear of the mansion; the others assaulted the front gate. The wooden door soon gave way, attacked as it was by a wooden beam which five or six of the men used as a battering ram. Now the silent night was rent with shouts and screams, and I dared go a little nearer. My master and Hara and Mase stayed outside the building, all with drawn swords, should Kira try to escape. The night was so still I could clearly hear the sound of swords hitting swords and the screams of those who were wounded. The noise had woken the people in the neighboring houses, and some, hastily clad, had come out into the street to see what was happening. Luckily for me, this allowed me to come even closer without being seen. Because of his greediness Kira

was not a popular man, and everyone understood immediately what was the cause of the noise of battle.

"I hope they catch the rat," a man near me exclaimed, but another said, "Rats have many holes to hide in." Looking at the excited expressions on their faces, I thought that Lord Kira's greed had left him no friends at all. No one likes a man who takes bribes, even though many pay them.

I saw Hara Soemon go inside the mansion. The plan was that when Kira was caught a whistle was to be blown, but so far no such sound had been heard. I moved a little closer; now I could make out the expression on my master's face. It was stern, the sternness of despair.

"Not yet." Hara Soemon had come back. "They are searching everywhere," he said.

"Has anyone been killed?" Oishi-sama was looking toward the gate as if he expected Lord Kira to walk out through it.

"There are many dead, the floor is slippery with blood; two of ours have received slight wounds, but none has been killed."

"If we have been robbed of our victory, then it would be better if we had died . . . He must be in the house." At that very moment, a whistle was heard. It sounded loud, for now the noises of battle had ceased.

My master smiled. I had drawn so close that I could almost reach out to touch him, and I did not like the smile — it did not enhance but disfigured his face.

"Come," he shouted and ran toward the gate. The others followed and so did I, for I had lost all sense of my station.

A servant boy had no right to mix in an affair like this, but no one noticed me.

In the large hall in the mansion, among the corpses strewn everywhere, knelt an old man; his white silken sleeping-robe had been torn from his shoulder, revealing a scar.

"That is the wound our master gave him," Yoshida Chuzaemon said as he pointed to the scar.

Holding his hands, palm against palm, in front of him, Oishi-sama bowed deeply, honoring the wound his master had given his enemy. The old man looked up at him as if he did not understand what was happening. Then, as he held out his hands the way a beggar would, my master killed him. Since it was Hazama Jujiro who had discovered Kira hiding in a closet, Oishi-sama gave him the honor of cutting off his head. The young samurai — he had seen but twenty-three winters — swung his sword and with one blow parted head from body. All the Asano ronin gave a shout of triumph, repeating it three times. In a corner of the room I saw a group of frightened women and children. The sight of them reminded me that I had no right to be there, and quickly I escaped outside again. Here the crowd had multiplied, but it was ordinary townspeople; I saw no samurai among them. Lord Kira's son had been adopted by the Uesugi family, and was now head of that famous clan. He had many retainers, who were supposed to be the best archers in Japan; I half expected them to come charging now. It had stopped snowing and the clouds had parted, revealing a star-filled sky, but in the east a faint light told that it would soon be morning.

Someone struck a gong, and now all the Ako ronin assem-

bled outside the house. Oishi-sama called their names and all could answer; none had lost their lives, and only two were slightly wounded.

The crowd that had assembled watched silently, filled with awe at the spectacle they were seeing. One of the ronin held high on a spear the head of Lord Kira. It was wrapped in a sleeve from his silken gown. On a word of command from my master the forty-seven true retainers of Ako formed ranks and marched toward Sengakuji temple, where Lord Asano their master was buried.

It was now the morning of the fifteenth, the day of the month when the lords who resided in Edo made their calls of courtesy at the Shogun's palace. Soon people would be up and about, but still the town was silent. As the samurai departed, some of the spectators returned to their house, but a few followed the marching men at a safe distance.

As we got nearer the temple, the stars in the sky faded as the light in the east grew stronger. At the temple gates most of the people who had followed stopped, but I didn't. I felt that I somehow had a right to see the end of that night's work. Still I was careful to hide as best I could, and in the shadow of a gravestone near Lord Asano's tomb I knelt down.

Oishi-sama, my master, was burning incense on a stone in front of the tomb. There he had placed a dagger, its hilt in the direction of the grave, the blade pointing toward the head of Kira. He retired a step or two and knelt on the ground, at the same time bowing his head low. Then he spoke to his Lord, telling him that he was sorry that he had not been able to have the house of Asano restored to the

rolls of nobility. He reported the deed they had done that night, as if it were not a snow-covered stone he was talking to but his Lord. At last my master rose. Taking the dirk, he struck the head of Kira three times, his arm in this act becoming the arm of his lord. The other Asano samurai ritually took the dagger and each struck the severed head of their enemy once. The act of revenge was completed.

Now all went into the temple to rest. As the last of them disappeared I stepped out from my hiding place. Now the head of Kira and the dagger were gone, but the smoke from incense rose, circling in the still air. I was about to turn and go when a voice near me said, "I saw you, urchin, following us." Otaka Gengo was standing right behind me. "If your master had seen you he might have chopped your head off as well."

I bowed my head as I mumbled, "I know it was not right but I had to see the end of it."

"Well, now it is over, and you have seen it, so go your way, child. Go to your riverside and play."

The words stung me, for I had loved Otaka Gengo and dreamed that he might be my father. As I looked up at him my eyes filled with tears, and I could feel them running down my cheeks. "Goodbye," I whispered and prepared to go.

"Hold on, boy." Otaka Gengo's arm shot out and caught hold of my shoulder. "This is no way for friends to part." When I turned my tear-stained face toward him, the samurai was smiling. "Jiro, the play is over; what will happen now is of little importance. When you act us, remember that we were never important; it was the deed we did that was." Otaka Gengo let go of my shoulder and gently pushed me in the direction of the temple gate. There I stopped and looked back; the samurai was still watching me. I waved my hand and he waved back and then I ran as fast as I could to the inn, collected my few belongings, and left for Kyoto. As the morning sun illuminated the snow-covered landscape, I was already in the outskirts of Edo.

Epilogue:
The End of the Story

"Would you have done it?" I looked across the little table at Chikamatsu.

He smiled and asked, "Would you?" I had just described to the playwright everything that had happened in Edo. We were sitting in the little soba shop where we had first met.

"No, I would not." I shook my head. "But then I am not a samurai."

"And neither am I." Chikamatsu-san picked up the last of his noodles, dipped it into the sauce, and ate it.

"Lord Asano had more than two hundred samurai in his service, but only forty-seven avenged him." I had hardly touched my dish. Now I ate a little while I thought how to phrase what I wanted to say. "I understand the others, the ones who said no, yet I don't really want to be counted among them."

"The heroic is always the more attractive, isn't it? No man dreams himself a coward." The playwright emptied his sake pitcher into his cup and gave a sign to order more. "It is part of my craft to understand them, both those who said yes and those who said no."

"But I felt sorry for Kira, when I saw him kneeling in his nightclothes. Yet he was an evil man; he deserved to be killed."

"Man is always quick to condemn and some are even eager to play executioner." Chikamatsu-san poured fresh sake from the pitcher brought him. "You need not be ashamed of feeling sorry for Kira; if the audience didn't, then it would have been a bad production." The playwright smiled. "I rather think the one you witnessed was a good one."

"Now they all have been condemned to commit seppuku. That is the end of the play." I drank the tea I had ordered; it was cold.

"No, the play ended with Kira's death. The seppuku is an epilogue that will never be performed. Forty-seven people slashing their bellies at the same time, the audience would laugh, or — even worse — grow bored."

"But then," I said eagerly, "they need not have done it?"

"Oh, they had to, or the play would have been an indifferent comedy. Inu-kubo, our Shogun, may be mad but not that mad; he proved himself no mean playwright when he condemned them to death." Chikamatsu-san laughed softly. "The play ends with Kira's death, as I said, but the knowledge that the triumphant samurai you see on the stage are actually dead men gives a depth to the scene which is necessary for the tragic ending. Each man loves that flame of life within him; even when he is old and it flickers, he will imagine well enough the hero's seppuku, but that scene must take place inside his mind."

"Otaka Gengo said that if I wanted to become an actor,

I would have to learn to creep inside another's soul. He also said that he thought that actors had none."

Chikamatsu-san nodded. "Your samurai friend is right on both accounts; it is a pity that he could not be spared."

"I was very fond of him." For a moment I pictured Otaka-sama in my mind.

"He seemed to have been worth caring for." Chikamatsu-san nodded sympathetically.

"He said I should go and serve a merchant, and that the time of the samurai was over."

"Yes, I agree, their time is finished, but not on the stage." Chikamatsu laughed. "There I think it is just beginning. Will you become a servant of a merchant?"

"No." I shook my head. "I want to become" — I paused and then whispered — "a riverside beggar."

Chikamatsu poured himself some more sake. "A riverside beggar. It is long since I have heard that phrase."

"My father was one, he came to Ako and they performed on the riverbank there; then they left. My mother cannot even remember his name, only that he was handsome."

Chikamatsu looked at me for a long time, then said, "You will do, I think. A pity you are not a little taller . . . Tell me, can you read and write?"

"I am learning it; a young monk is teaching me. He says that I am not too clumsy with the brush, but he has been paid to teach me and it might not be true."

"I have need of someone to help me at times. You said your name is Jiro? Well, Jiro, would you serve me? I do not think you will grow rich from it, but there are a few things I could teach you."

"Oh my lord, I will, I will!" I bowed so low my head banged on the table.

"Master, not lord. The samurai can keep their lofty titles. By all means bow, but do not knock all sense out of your head by bowing so low."

Chikamatsu rose and paid and left the little inn. I followed him, stepping into a new life now that the old one was over.